Snow Signs

by
Jennifer Seet

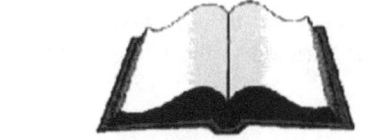

CCB Publishing
British Columbia, Canada

Snow Signs

Library and Archives Canada Cataloguing in Publication

Seet, Jennifer, 1946-
Snow Signs / written by Jennifer Seet.
ISBN 978-0-9809995-9-4
I. Title.
PS3619.E356S66 2008   813'.6   C2008-903464-3

Publisher: CCB Publishing
              British Columbia, Canada
              www.ccbpublishing.com

Dedicated to my daughter-in-law, Jen
and my 'sister' Candace.
The women in this book have qualities I admire.
I see the same qualities in both of you!

ACKNOWLEDGMENTS

My dear husband of forty years, Bob, gave me the idea for this book. He has been a staunch supporter of my writing for the time I've been at it full force.

I also want to thank my family for having faith in me. Without their love and patience, I couldn't do it.

I decided to write about a deaf woman because of my experience in teaching at the Indiana School for the Deaf. During my thirty years there, I would write a Christmas story for my co-workers that always included a deaf theme. They seemed to enjoy them and encouraged me to continue doing so after retirement. This is my way of thanking them for their support too.

I would like to thank First Sgt. Brian Olehy for giving me invaluable information about the rankings, job responsibilities and inner workings of the Indiana State Police force.

I would also like to credit the deputies at my lake community for helping me understand the regulations of living on "Sweetwater".

My first book, *Borderland*, took advantage of a paranormal interest I have had since childhood. This book carries on that interest. Thank you to all of my readers who enjoy and believe!

PROLOGUE

A fine feathery mist of snow filtered down through a stand of winter-barren timber. Few drops landed on the outstretched naked branches, but by morning, as intensity increased, a thick coating would illuminate the landscape, much like the full moon now shining in the night sky.

Light from the moon streaked through the austere woods, casting a silvery surreal tinge to everything in its path. Mimicking the brush strokes on an artist's canvas, it left a lasting impression of visual imagery, both symbolic and real. For a lone figure stood mutely in the shadow of the trees, her whiteness sharply contrasted but strangely absorbed by the surroundings.

She watched a house, hoping to find someone staring back at her, but no one did. The windows were darkened; shades were drawn; only darkness reflected from within.

But, if someone had been inside, gazing out into the stark black and white of the cold night, that person could have been at first curious, and then concerned for this fragile waif, alone, without benefit of coat, gloves, or hat, braving the icy chill, showing no signs of hypothermia, no shivering, not even a hint of discomfort.

Further, leaning forward, and on closer inspection, the observer might have come to understand that there was something different about the solitary being out in the snow. And, a sharp intake of breath would have accompanied a realization that whatever it was standing in the woods, it was too transparent to be real. Perhaps it was only murky obscurity playing tricks on the mind?

Then, a gasp might have formed in the throat, catching in the back, struggling to come out as the watcher could have seen something red materialize and trickle down from bony white fingertips. Slowly, it would have become apparent that it was blood dripping on the ground, not too much, just enough to leave a bright-red stain on the snowy blanket.

And, if that person would have looked up in time, it might have been obvious, but not yet comprehensible, that the figure had already vanished into the night.

CHAPTER ONE

Birds flocked to the new birdfeeder, brilliant red cardinals, a black and white-breasted chickadee, all in sharp contrast to the snow-covered landscape and sterile trees.

Claire watched, a smile forming on her face. *Good*, she thought, *first purchase for my new retirement home and it's a hit with the birds.*

She stood there, ramrod straight, hypnotized by the beauty of the nature in her front yard. A tall, slender woman, she exhibited the erect posture of a self-confident person, used to being in a position of authority… and in a uniform. Her hair was still a soft light blonde with flecks of white beginning to peek through, and her eyes were almost a copper color in their brilliance. She had womanly curves, inviting to any male, but showing the softer side of a female on the other side of fifty. Her hands were graceful, her fingers long and delicate.

Men had often complimented her on her beautiful hands, probably imagining how they would feel stroking their faces, soft to the touch but passionate as well.

Frost on the window was beginning to cloud her vision so she had to squint to see the cardinals and the chickadee more clearly. Her breath formed opaque circles on the glass and further impeded her vision, so she wrapped her arms around her chest and began to move away, shivering in response to the cold outside.

But, as she retreated, out of the corner of her eye she noticed a slight movement, and when she turned around, she saw the wind pick up the snow and send it swirling into the air.

How beautiful, she thought. *I have a winter wonderland outside my front door and don't have to leave the house to enjoy it!*

"There are some perks to being retired, Claire Dungarvan! No phone calls at 3:00 a.m. No fighting traffic to get to a crime scene. No more psychos to deal with."

Letting out a soft chuckle, she walked towards the kitchen to get a cup of coffee. Delicately fingering the hot cup in one hand, she picked up the newspaper with the other and moved toward the living room again to enjoy the outdoor scenery.

As she sat down on the couch, she glanced over at the picture window one more time and her instinct for detail told her that something was different. It was like something was out of place, not the same as before.

Claire saw the birds flocking around the feeder, shrugged her shoulders, and tried to concentrate on the newspaper. But after reading the headline for the fifth time, she slammed the paper down and stood up to get a closer look.

Damn! Am I ever going to enjoy myself?

Thirty years of police work had made her more than just a little observant. It could be a nuisance at times when she was trying to concentrate on something else, and that's how it felt now. Compelled to see what was awry in the tranquil scene of a few minutes ago, she couldn't just enjoy the view; she had to analyze it.

She looked at the birds…nothing amiss. The cardinals and the chickadee continued to enjoy their new feeding spot. Her lips twitched, suppressing a grin. *Looks like the squirrels have discovered the bird feeder too!*

Then, her eyes traveled across the front yard, lingering on the spot in between the trees where she had seen the snow swirling around.

Nothing there now, she thought.

But as she started to turn back towards the couch, she stopped. *Wait a minute! There is something different!*

Turning around to give it another look, her trained eyes took in all the surroundings. No movement. But when she gazed down at the ground, she noticed a spot right below where the snow had blown up.

"How peculiar", she said aloud. "It almost looks like….what?" Leaning closer to the windowpane, her breathing began to cloud her vision again.

"I can't quite make it out." Straining to bring the spot into focus, she stared intently, her breath catching in her throat.

Finally exhaling, she proclaimed, "This is ridiculous!"

She moved away from the window and sat back down. "I've been retired for a week and I'm already talking to myself!"

Letting out another big sigh, she forced herself to relax, and sipping her coffee, allowed her mind to wander.

A lifetime of service with the Indiana state police, the first ten years as a trooper and the next ten as a senior trooper, and then the final ten of her total thirty years on the force as a detective trooper, had made Claire a very suspicious person.

Suspicious? Maybe that's not the word. But, observant? Yes, for sure.

Definitely not rich, or married for that matter, she thought. *I never had time for relationships! Oh sure, once or twice I was close enough to entertain the idea of settling down.* And, a bittersweet smile crossed her face when she remembered her first true love.

Doug was a fellow state trooper. A shy, boyish type, he had the strong muscular build of a weight lifter, an oxymoron of a statement, but one that fit him to a tee. He loved her with all his heart and he wanted to marry, but he also wanted the dream stay-at-home wife.

Claire couldn't see herself doing that. She was young and ambitious, definitely not ready for any commitment that might stand in the way of her career.

So, they ended their brief romance on a positive note and moved on, no looking back, no letting it interfere with their working relationship.

At least that's what we told each other! She dipped her head and glanced at the newspaper. She briefly entertained the thought of reading once again, but knew that she needed to finish what she started, so she braved the pain and resumed her thoughts.

❖

And then there had been Greg. He had seemed different than other men she had dated, nice, maybe a little controlling, but nothing she had time to really put her finger on. She met him while Christmas shopping at the mall, where they both wound up at Blake and Norris bookstore, sharing a table as they sipped coffee and read their purchases.

"This place is crowded. Mind if I sit with you?" a voice had asked.

She had been attracted immediately to his gorgeous eyes--sea-green.

God! You could swim in them!

Right then and there she was instantly intrigued and wanted to get to know this man better. When he sat down after ordering his drink, she couldn't help but notice the determined set of his jaw, the strong, lean lines of his body. He exuded male hormones.

He immediately started flipping through his book, which she noticed was by an author she enjoyed too. But when she went back to reading her purchase, Claire quickly recognized and accepted the fact that her concentration was broken. She'd read a paragraph, look up, read another paragraph, glance over. Once or twice she observed that he was looking at her, too.

Finally, their eyes locked and laughing, they realized they were more interested in each other than in what they were reading. So, they shoved the books aside and began to talk. It didn't take them long to understand that they had a lot more in common than just the mutual attraction. Claire found Greg knowledgeable about a number of subjects and easy to engage in conversation.

He asked her to dinner for that next Saturday. She accepted readily. They became better acquainted on their first date and started seeing as much of each other as their busy schedules would allow in the following weeks.

"Played out like a bad novel...boy meets girl; girl gets her hopes up..."

I really opened up to him, telling him about Doug...but, he didn't share much of value with me…and, unfortunately, he never shared that he was married. Claire still blanched every time she remembered that part.

She found out one day while standing in one of the aisles of the very same Blake and Norris bookstore when she heard a familiar voice talking to a female, "Hey hon, are you ready to leave yet?"

Claire peered around the end of the aisle and saw Greg. Confused, she looked closer to make sure it really was him, and that's when she noticed the shiny gold of a wedding band on his finger.

"Just let me pay for this book and I'll be done," the woman responded.

And, Claire noted a ring on her finger, blazing with a sparkly brilliance that announced to the entire world that he was her man and she was his woman.

Claire stood there frozen with shock, but hidden from view, until Greg and his wife left the bookstore.

After that, when he called (*and he did call—more than a few times!*), she never answered the phone or returned his messages. She could have checked into his background a little more at the time, but she was embarrassed and didn't want to know anything else about him.

It was a dead issue to me—over—I was too ashamed to find out anymore.

Finally he stopped trying to contact her altogether. *Probably knew his little secret was out…or maybe he just found another unsuspecting victim,* she fumed.

Even though it was more than a few years ago, tears formed in her eyes, remembering this particularly painful time. It still hurt and was probably the reason she never committed to a serious relationship again. At the time her career as a detective trooper was in full swing and she devoted herself entirely to her job.

When she made detective ten years ago, Claire felt she had

finally reached the pinnacle of her career. She had always found herself fascinated with the crime scene, literally pulled into the details of the investigation, even though she didn't have the final authority or credentials to do more until she felt brave enough to apply for an opening in that division.

Luckily, her supervisor, Corporal George Stanley, had seen this attention to detail, the interest in gathering evidence, and the ability to communicate with witnesses until she intractably drew them into her confidence. That's why Corporal Stanley didn't hesitate to recommend her to the "Chief" when she came to see him in his office.

Captain Marvin Hennessey, the division commander at the time, had known Claire since she started on the force and had always wanted to give her a chance, but she had graciously turned him down for other promotional assignments in the hope that something would open up in the detective division.

"Chief, I'm just not ready yet," she would tell him.

Everyone called Marvin "Chief". It seemed like even before he became a Captain he was called 'Chief'. Marvin didn't demand this title out of respect; he just earned it. And in everyone's minds, he was the Chief long before he was promoted to the rank of Captain.

"Claire, just tell me when you're ready. We'll make room for you if we have to."

"I know Chief. I'll let you know."

But even as she gained more experience and honed her investigative skills, she waited her turn. She didn't want to usurp anyone's position. That was always the way Claire operated: unassuming, professional, and respectful of others.

Then when Bernie Olson announced his retirement ten years ago, she knew the time was right and put in her application the next day.

George Stanley read the paperwork while she stood by waiting for a response.

Looking up finally, he said, "What took you so long!"

Smiling, Claire recalled all the times when the two of them met in this office, going over accident reports and other business together. "Just couldn't bring myself to do it, George. I knew I would miss the direct contact I have with you."

He chuckled but grew quiet as he thought about how much he enjoyed having her work specifically with him and how much he would miss the everyday shared camaraderie.

"You're a good senior trooper, Claire, but you deserve this chance…and we'll still be working together. You know you can come to me any time."

Shaking hands, she noticed that he held on a little longer than normal. She knew that when she left the office, there would be a tinge of sadness overshadowing the excitement…for both of them.

As she turned and faced the door, she stopped and considered the possibility of grabbing the application out of George's hand. She shook her head. *No, I need this opportunity. No turning back now.*

He watched the hesitation and headshake from behind his desk and was tempted to ask her to reconsider. George knew the challenges that lay ahead for her. But he knew Claire well enough to know she was up to the demands of the new job. Self-doubts would soon give way to self-confidence.

"Good luck to you, Claire," he called out as she quietly shut the door.

Of course, Chief wasted no time in approving her application and announced the promotion to detective the very next week. No one was surprised, but there was still grumbling from some of the patrol troopers about a 'woman detective'. Even during the mid-1990's there was a sexist attitude prevalent in the state police rank and file, especially in southern Indiana.

Claire knew what was going on and she worked diligently to dispel any doubts about her ability; she worked harder and longer hours than anyone to gain the respect of her fellow detectives and the trust of the road officers in her new capacity as well.

It didn't take long for them to realize that she was very competent and adept at combing crime and accident scenes for clues and evidence to help derive answers that others couldn't or wouldn't see.

Soon, she found herself being called on to help with some sticky crimes, ones that had more questions than answers.

As Claire found herself reliving this part of her past, she thought about one crime in particular that had always haunted her...the disappearance of a young deaf woman, as yet unsolved.

CHAPTER TWO

Her name was Libby Newman and she was never found even though police suspected murder. They investigated her ex-husband for a while but couldn't get enough evidence either physical or circumstantial to arrest him, let alone come to the conclusion that it was an actual crime. *No body, no evidence of a struggle at the house, no leads*.

And, the only thing Claire had was a lingering suspicion that Libby was murdered. There were footprints leading from the house, two sets. One set obviously belonged to a woman. The other set was larger and likely belonged to a man, but were never matched to a suspect's shoes. They led to a dead end…literally. A power station close to Libby's house was where the trail stopped. There was a cement walkway in front of the station and the prints ended there.

Of course, Claire took impressions of the shoe prints, but they didn't have any discriminating marks on them that would give her a lead.

The smaller ones were identified as Libby's through a search of her closet and a relative's accounting of what was missing. The clothes she had on and her tennis shoes were the only items gone from the house.

The other set was compared to the ex-husband's shoes and no match was found even though they were the same size. The shoes themselves were identified as size ten, typical average male size, common brand favored by many males, adults and youths, nothing distinguishing except that they were obviously new shoes, no unique tread on the soles. The person she went with knew enough not to use old shoes that might have a wear pattern on them.

Stores in the surrounding area were checked to see if anyone recognized the husband as buying shoes recently, but no one did. And, since he traveled a lot, he could have purchased them in any number of places.

But the shoes were not the only reason that Claire suspected Libby was murdered.

Someone went to a lot of trouble just to kidnap her. And…if she disappeared on her own, why hasn't she shown up in the last four years? Why wouldn't she contact her family, if only to tell them she was okay?

Since then, no one had spotted Libby or found a body matching her description. Claire had a feeling that the ex-husband knew more than he was telling.

But Mr. Newman talked with the other officer working the case and he gave him a solid alibi.

Trent Newman was a trucker and his company had records to back up his assertion that he was on the road, fifty miles from Libby's house, when she disappeared.

There were no domestic disturbance or abuse allegations from the marriage, no history of violence in what was known of his past. A few ex-girlfriends were interviewed but no one had dated him long enough to know him that well, even though some hinted that he seemed 'possessive' during the short time they were together. He always wanted to monopolize their time and sulked when they were not available.

The only thing Claire had to go on was a hunch. She just knew that Trent Newman had something to do with his ex-wife's disappearance, and she also suspected that he had killed her, but she didn't have the evidence to prove it.

"Well, enough of this!" Claire said, attempting to break her train of thought.

She jumped up from the couch, walked into the kitchen, and went over her plans for the day, while absentmindedly washing out her coffee cup and placing it in the dishwasher. She intended to spend time at the computer, writing.

Claire had always enjoyed writing, and since she started working for the state police, she had kept a journal and records of all of her cases. When she took early retirement, her secret desire was to write novels based on her experiences as a state policewoman.

As she walked into the front bedroom that doubled as her office, she thought about the fact that writing was a form of therapy for her, but it also kept her mind active and attuned to police work. For the first time since she made the decision to retire, she experienced a twinge of regret.

"Maybe I should have stayed on," Claire spoke aloud as she sat down at the computer.

No, she thought. *I was ready. I was beginning to feel the burnout so many policemen and women experience after years and years of taking care of victims, using restraint in the face of perpetrators, seeing the violence and never understanding why humans do such inhumane things to each other. I just need to write, because I can write about the ugly part of police work without having to feel it.*

Snickering, she said, "Who am I trying to kid!"

She pressed the button to start the computer, and, while it brought up where she had left off, Claire looked outside to see if any more birds were at the feeder. She had intentionally placed her computer in this room so she could enjoy the nature outside, but instead, her eyes moved across the yard to the spot where she had seen the blowing snow. Leaning forward to focus in on the area, what she saw made her flinch.

There is something there! Something red!

Claire pressed up against the computer to get as close to the window as she could.

It looks like blood!

She continued to peer out the window at the bright red dotting the snow and grunted in disgust at herself, realizing she wasn't going to get any writing done until she found out what it was.

Finally she stood up and stomped into the living room, pausing only long enough to grab her winter boots on the floor beside the front door.

She hastily shoved her feet into the boots and went out on the porch to get a better look.

It's blood, she realized, moving down the full length of the porch, clutching the railing and leaning over to see the red drops in the snow more clearly.

Must be an animal, she decided. *I bet a deer was injured and walked through the yard, dripping blood onto the snow. That has to be it!*

Claire had seen bucks, does, and their fawns in her yard just about every morning since moving here. Her neighbors across the street had a salt block and her yard was a natural pathway for the deer to get to their food source.

I'll have to ask Kate and Myra if they noticed any injured deer or blood drops in their yard.

Kate Lines and Myra Collier were two elderly ladies who lived across the street and they loved to bird watch and feed the animals.

Maybe they noticed the blood too.

Claire continued to stare at the droplets…no form, no shape or symbol, just specks of blood, red against the white, hypnotizing in their mystery.

CHAPTER THREE

Disturbed by the blood in her front yard, but stymied as to why it was there, Claire forced herself to return to her computer and begin writing.

She had already decided to use the story of Libby Newman as the basis for her first novel, but as she started to put down the details, she found herself returning to the blood in the snow. It almost felt as if the drops were connected to Libby in some way.

That's silly, she thought. *My mind's on her and that's why I'm feeling this way.*

She plodded on with the writing, but had to stop several times as she found herself going over the details of the case, and the reasons why she found it so fascinating in the first place.

Four years ago when Libby Newman disappeared, she and her husband, Trent, had been divorced for a year. There was nothing in the divorce decree that indicated any past violence or threats to her. The property was split fairly evenly and Libby kept the house. Nothing showed up in that year to indicate that Trent was upset about any of the terms of the divorce. He was often on the road, continuing to work for the same trucking company. It seemed as if he took more assignments farther away than in the past, but that was understandable.

Maybe he just wanted to be by himself for a while and think things through. Or, maybe he didn't want to be close enough to be reminded of the life he had had while married to Libby.

At any rate, Claire reasoned, *there were no police reports logged by the ex-wife after the divorce, not even a hint that he might be trying to contact her.*

When interviewed, her family members didn't have much to

say about the divorce. At first they had been concerned about Libby's emotional state, but they soon realized that she was adapting and seemed to enjoy living on her own.

If pressed, they might have been too embarrassed to admit that they didn't have very good signing skills, and therefore, they really didn't know how she felt about her now ex-husband and the divorce.

As for who might have wanted to harm her, no one knew Libby well enough to even venture a guess. She was a private person; she didn't share her fears or dreams with others.

Maybe she decided to go off and find a better life…but that's only speculation on my part.

Being an isolated person with few friends and no neighbors close by, eyebrows were raised when she married Trent in the first place, but no one was willing to admit that they had not taken the time to get to know this beautiful young woman better.

They met at the local high school where they both had signed up for an adult education computer class. He noticed the interpreter the first night of class and was immediately fascinated by the interaction and communication between the two of them. He had a deaf childhood friend in his neighborhood when he was growing up and had learned minimal sign language for when they played together, but he had not used it in a long time.

Trent frowned when he remembered how his friend's mother decided she didn't want her son playing with him anymore. *She thought I wasn't a good 'influence' on him.* Trent shook his head. *He never would tell me why his Mom didn't like me.*

Increasingly interested, he turned his attention back to Libby and her interpreter. In the next few weeks, he watched unobtrusively before deciding to go up and introduce himself one night after class.

Libby had been watching him too and was impressed with his basic signing skills and touched by his willingness to communicate directly with her instead of depending on the interpreter, when he finally did introduce himself.

Not bad looking, a little older than me, but that's okay, she thought.

Trent was of medium build, about five feet, eleven inches tall, and he had kept his weight under control, unlike a lot of truckers. His dark brown hair helped bring out the light flecks of gold in his brown eyes, offering a pleasing contrast, and he had a nice smile, even though others might have remarked on the cruel twist it sometimes provided.

But Libby only saw the good side of Trent, and soon the two of them were going out for coffee after class, and it wasn't long before they were dating. He did not sign well enough to get into any deep conversations with her, but she found herself attracted to him and eventually she fell in love.

In retrospect friends and family might have questioned whether this relationship could last, but Libby was lonesome and stubborn. She wanted to marry Trent and settle down. She didn't know him that well, but in her mind that was fine.

They eloped to Las Vegas, and after they came back, Libby and Trent decided to buy the little house in the country she had been renting, and they both returned to their normal lives.

Libby went back to work at Glenco, a plastics manufacturing company located close by in the small town of Frederick. She held onto her dream of transferring from the factory to the office, but hadn't accomplished that feat even when she disappeared.

Trent went back to driving a truck, the only job he had ever known.

Life seemed normal for the newly-married couple, but no one really knew what went on inside that house.

No one had any idea there was trouble in the marriage until it was too late. The divorce attorneys used the standard argument, "irreconcilable differences", and neither party discussed it much beyond that.

After the divorce was final, Libby became more of a loner and family members mistakenly thought she just needed time to come to grips with everything. If they had asked her, they might have been surprised, because Libby had known almost from the beginning that the marriage was in trouble.

She had heard that sometimes hearing men married deaf women so they could be possessive, be the 'boss' of the family. She didn't really see that in Trent at first because he tried so hard; he was in love with her and thrilled that she felt the same about him.

But, as time went by, Libby saw the other side of Trent Newman. She saw in him the desire to control every aspect of her life, including what she wore, whom she had as friends, where she went, and how long she stayed out.

Finally it got so bad that Libby just stopped seeing other people and came straight home from work, especially when Trent was there.

Friends and family members were worried but finally just accepted it. They thought she wanted to be with her husband.

Little did they know that she was too proud to admit her marriage was a mistake. She tried to hide her disappointment from others, but she couldn't hide it for long. Finally, she asked for the divorce.

He reluctantly agreed, but only after months of arguing, attempted persuading, verbal abuse, veiled threats, and false accusations.

When she went through with it, Trent accepted the fact, *or at least that is what other people thought.* He even had Libby fooled into believing that he had come to terms with the divorce.

That's why no one could have suspected him of having anything to do with her disappearance. He had moved on.

But had he? Claire wondered about that and always questioned if the divorce had anything to do with what happened to Libby. *Revenge? Was it motivation to harm her? Did it affect him more than others realized?*

She had seen it before, many times. A couple divorced; one of them held a grudge; someone got hurt and someone was responsible for it. Claire shook her head and tried to concentrate on her writing but couldn't get one thought out of her mind, the thought that Trent Newman knew exactly what had happened to his ex-wife.

CHAPTER FOUR

Morning sunlight streamed in the bedroom window causing Claire to open her eyes slowly and look around, still not believing that she could sleep as long as she wanted, let alone until daylight.

Most of the time when she was working, Claire was up before dawn, preparing for the day, if she was lucky. If she wasn't lucky, she would receive a phone call in the middle of the night requesting her presence at an accident site, crime scene, or if she was truly unlucky, at a homicide.

Today it took her a while to make sense of the surroundings and to come to the realization that she was indeed retired and no longer a slave to the morning routine she had become so accustomed to while working.

Ring! Ring! The telephone blared out a sound so loud as to disrupt any idea she might have had about going back to sleep.

She rolled over, picked up the receiver and answered rather drowsily, "Hello."

"Claire, it's George. Glad I caught you before you left the house to do whatever you retired people do."

"Very funny, George. If you couldn't tell by my voice, I'm just waking up…and it feels wonderful, I might add." She held the phone out away from her ear, anticipating his boisterous reprimand.

"Be careful, woman. I might just send someone over there to throw you out of bed. Or, maybe I'll just come and do it myself," he added.

Claire had to laugh, "Yeah, I bet you would. So, why are you calling so early? I haven't even had that first cup of coffee."

"Don't rub it in, Missy or I will come over!"

Chuckling, he continued, "No, I was calling to talk to you about Chief's retirement party…wanted to know if you were coming, and if so, would you say a few things. You know, like

18

how many times he saved your ass, kept you out of trouble, that kind of thing...but keep it clean, his wife will be there."

"Oh, like Mary doesn't already know what a cantankerous old fart he is!"

"Guess he didn't have you fooled either, huh," George laughed.

"Not much," she replied, adding, "Sure, I'll be there and plan to say a few things. Seven o'clock tomorrow night, right?"

"Yeah, and don't be late." George smiled because he knew this would get a rile out of her.

"What do you mean 'late'? I was never late...unlike some of my good ol' boy co-workers on the force, I might add."

She said a quick 'goodbye' and hung up before he could come back with another retort.

Claire sat on the side of the bed and organized her plans for the day. *First order of business is to make some coffee!*

She found herself humming "When Irish Eyes Are Smiling" as she walked to the kitchen, and it truly matched her frame of mind. Claire was happy for the first time in a long time. She looked forward to seeing everyone tomorrow night, sharing old stories, catching up on all the news, and just enjoying the company.

That's one thing she missed about working--the camaraderie of group interaction on a daily basis. She needed to get out more and find other social outlets, but for now she was content to be by herself, writing and appreciating the nature around her.

As she poured the water in the coffee pot, she thought, *speaking of nature, wonder if the birds have enough seed?*

Claire turned on the coffee and went to the living room window. But when she looked outside, her eyes didn't immediately go to the bird feeder. Instead, she looked at the place in the snow where she saw the blood yesterday.

What she saw there caused a sharp intake of breath, followed by her grabbing onto the wall for support.

More blood was evident, and something else was there too...*it...it looks like footprints!*

She struggled to regain her composure as her analytical mind made some quick observations.

The blood looked fresh and there was more of it. If it was an animal, chances are one of her neighbors would find it soon...and it would be seriously wounded or dead, because the amount of blood was significant.

The footprints (or shoeprints to be exact) were a mystery.

Did someone find an injured deer in my yard and shoot it?

If so, I would have heard it, she determined.

I'm so attuned to gunshots that I would have heard one even in a deep sleep. And, if someone shot a deer, why would that person take a chance on doing it here?

Claire lived in an area of homes close to two lakes called a Conservancy. It was governed by a locally elected group of neighbors and had its own set of rules and regulations. She knew they included no hunting or shooting within the boundaries.

Plus, I don't see any dragging marks in the snow to indicate that someone took the deer with him.

Strange...Well, I'll put on my boots, go out and have a look myself, she decided. *I have to go to the mailbox and get the paper anyway.*

Wait a minute! Claire paused and remembered something.

"I didn't see any blood yesterday morning when I got the paper."

But, it was there just a little while later when I was reading the paper, she reminded herself. *How did I miss an injured deer in such a short time frame?*

"And, of course the prints weren't there yesterday."

Perplexed, she walked over to pour herself some coffee. *Maybe the caffeine will help clear my head and...* "I can think better," she said the last part aloud.

"Oh, what the heck! Might as well fix myself a big breakfast to go with the coffee."

Claire's lips turned up into a slight smile and she shook her head at the recent increasing propensity she had developed for talking to herself. *I'd better be careful or before you know it, people will begin to think I have dementia!*

She pulled out the frying pan and tried to concentrate on other matters. She thought about other details of the Libby Newman case that she wanted to include in her writing.

Never did find any evidence to link her ex-husband to the disappearance, she remembered.

At first, the police wondered if it was a kidnapping, but no ransom note or phone call ever came to the family.

Once they checked the trucking company and realized that Trent Newman was miles away when his wife went missing, they started to look at other friends and family members.

No one stood out. Everyone loved Libby, and everyone was at a loss as to what happened to her. Of course there was always the possibility that she had left of her own accord.

But why didn't she take anything with her? And, she lived alone; she was vulnerable; it happened at night; she lived in an isolated area. Did she want it to look like someone kidnapped her so she could disappear off the face of the earth? If someone helped her, why hasn't he come forward after all this time?

All these facts led investigators to wonder if anyone would ever be charged with a crime—if in fact any wrongdoing had been committed. Some assumed she had just run off, upset by the broken promises from the marriage… and the job.

It was known that Libby was very disappointed when she never received a promotion at work. She challenged management to give her a chance. She had been taking courses in adult education and had an associate's degree in business management from State Business College.

But even with the diploma, Libby found it difficult to get her employer to recognize her capabilities. She always wondered if it was because of her deafness and the fact that people didn't know how to communicate with her.

It might have made her sad enough to just up and leave, disappear, and find a better place, one that would accept her and give her more opportunities.

Maybe she just wanted to put her past behind... for the hope of a better future, Claire speculated. *And, maybe with her marriage dissolved, she felt it was time.*

Claire placed the sizzling bacon and fried egg on a plate. *If so, why would she leave in the middle of the night, taking nothing with her? She didn't have anything to hide.*

Placing the frying pan back on the stove, Claire grabbed the coffee pot and poured herself another cup.

Her house certainly didn't look like someone planned to move. Everything was in its place. She only had the clothes on her back.

Claire sat down at the table and cut her egg into pieces.

Her purse was even on the kitchen table. That was the strangest part...no sign of struggle, but also no indication of a designed outing. It was like she just vanished.

"I wish I could talk to her so I could know what happened that night." Claire spoke into the air around her as she blew on her hot coffee.

"Strong possibility she's not living anymore and likely I'll never know what happened."

Claire got up to put some bread in the toaster and thought about what else puzzled her.

Witnesses had seen Trent Newman's truck at a Circle Y truck stop about 50 miles from Libby's house that night. It had been parked there for a few hours before anyone noticed that Trent was nowhere to be seen. When questioned, he said that he had climbed up into his sleeping compartment. He was returning from a long trip, had become sleepy, and decided not to drive the last miles to his house without taking a nap. He was afraid that he might have an accident, and that is why he pulled off there in the first place.

No one had looked in the truck. If they had, maybe all they would have seen was the curtain drawn with the seam of a blanket hanging out from underneath. It sure would have looked like someone was sleeping, not an uncommon sight at a truck stop.

Someone did report seeing a man boarding a motorcycle parked close to the truck earlier that evening, but that was not an unusual sight either.

The man was medium build, had on jeans and a t-shirt, and he also had long hair, peeking out from underneath his helmet, altogether nothing much to go on, and nothing to bring suspicion on Trent.

When questioned, others couldn't remember seeing the motorcyclist, and the witness didn't think to get the license number.

Later on that night Trent did come into the diner to have a bite to eat. He said he had overslept and was in a hurry to get home. He'd been on the road for five days and was anxious to have some time off. He ate a big meal and left.

No one noticed anything suspicious about his appearance. His clothes were rumpled but not dirty...or bloody. His shoes were clean and his short-cropped hair was not out of place.

Everything about his appearance backed up his story that he took a nap and was on his way home from a long trip.

Truck stops are mobile places; people come and go. Sometimes the pace of the activity makes it difficult to remember any details.

Certainly no one would have noticed if the motorcycle came back...and happened to be parked in the same spot, next to the truck.

The only people who would have seen it were working their shifts at the truck stop...and they didn't have time to notice, let alone wonder if it was even the same motorcycle...or the same truck.

CHAPTER FIVE

"Well, time to get started," Claire said aloud as she washed the dishes and put them in the drainer.

She ran a washcloth over the countertop and table, making sure the kitchen was clean and back to normal before going outside to check on the blood and shoeprints.

As she put her feet into her boots, she once again thought about the reappearing blood.

It's strange that it would just show up like that. Then overnight, more blood...doesn't make sense...and, why the prints?

All of these thoughts were going through her head when she opened the door and braced herself for the frigid air before walking out onto the front porch.

She walked down the steps and through the yard with her head down, a buffer from the stinging cold.

"Hey, Claire."

She looked up to see Myra pulled to a stop in front of the house. She had a newspaper in her hand.

"I thought you might want this. I decided to drive up and get my paper--didn't want to walk in the cold."

"Thanks, Myra. I was just going to get it." She came out to the car and took the extended newspaper.

She thanked her and started to turn around, but hesitated before asking, "Oh, by the way, did you see any injured deer in your yard yesterday or today?"

"Injured? No, can't say that I did. Why?"

"Well, see this blood," Claire turned and pointed to the drops in the snow. "It was here yesterday too. I was thinking that maybe a deer had been injured."

"Yeah, I see what you mean," Myra said as she squinted in the bright morning sun.

"But what are those footprints doing there? Did you notice them yesterday too?"

"No, that's the strangest part. Yesterday there was just a little blood, enough to make me think there might be an injured animal, maybe a deer. Today, I look out my window and see more blood and the prints! I have no idea where they came from."

"Well, just be careful. It looks like someone might have been in your yard and killed a deer. They're not supposed to do that here in the Conservancy, but that's what it looks like."

She paused and then asked, "Did you hear any shots?"

Claire shook her head 'no' and continued to stare at the blood.

With a puzzled look on her face, Myra asked, "Did you report it to the office yet?"

"No, not yet. I was just coming out to take a closer look. Do you think I should call?"

"I would if I were you. Have Jim Hoppes come and look at it. He's the sheriff's deputy who patrols the Conservancy. He can help."

"Yes, I know Jim. I've worked with him on a few cases and he's a good guy. I might just do that."

Claire wavered, as if thinking through her options before adding, "Thanks Myra. You take care and have a good day."

Myra waved as she pulled the Jeep into her driveway across the street.

Claire didn't want to alarm her but as she looked closer at the blood and shoeprints, she realized that it was just too 'pat'. There was only one set of prints, which was very strange since they didn't lead anywhere.

Why and how would someone leave only one set of shoeprints in a yard? And, if there were logical explanations, why would someone even try to hunt down an animal in a restricted neighborhood? There are always people around, looking out their window at anything suspicious. Even with the small stand of trees obscuring the view, surely someone would have seen or heard a hunter!

No, this didn't look like that to Claire. It looked almost staged; it looked like someone wanted her to see this...*and if so, why?*

Claire stared at the prints. *Tread looks like what you find on an athletic shoe, possibly size 10, no unusual tread. Wonder why the person didn't wear boots?*

Suddenly, she stopped and straightened up. A puzzled look came across her face. *Typical description of shoes,* she decided, *but one that I have thought about recently.*

Claire's heart beat a little faster. *Hold on! Same description as in the Libby Newman case! Same size shoeprints found at the site where she disappeared!*

Shivering in response to the cold air, but also because of the intriguing similarities, she decided, *No, it's just my imagination.*

So what! I've been thinking about that case, writing about it, and now I'm seeing it in the snow?

She smiled ruefully and turned to go back into the house. *Ridiculous! My brain hasn't caught up with my body yet on this retirement thing. My mind is still in detective mode and if I'm not careful, I'll lose it completely!*

But as Claire walked through the front door, she didn't see what formed in the snow behind her. If she had, she probably would have startled and jumped even though she was a seasoned detective, used to things that were strange and unusual.

Flakes of snow danced in the air, swirling faster and faster, growing into something formative, blurry, but resembling a person, without the substance of a human being, but mirroring a shadow or a ghost of someone long dead.

At least it would look like that to someone who believed in that kind of thing, but Claire wasn't a believer, not yet anyway.

CHAPTER SIX

Seated at the computer, Claire tried to come up with some remarks to make at Marvin's retirement party. Even though the party wasn't until tomorrow night, she wanted to prepare her speech, and writing was the best way for her to do that. She found that putting it down helped her to remember the details. That's why she had turned to writing as a hobby, and that's why she depended on it to help her now.

She thought back to all the times that Chief had been there for her. First and foremost he had taken a chance when he promoted her to detective, and she would always be grateful for that opportunity.

Smiling, she remembered how he jokingly told her his wife, Mary, would never speak to him again if he did not help Claire make detective. She knew he was only saying that to break the ice. He had heard some of the same complaints she had heard about a 'female in the ranks'.

He took her to lunch with the other detectives from her post right after the promotion was announced. He did it so that they could get to know her better and realize what an asset she would be to the division.

Chief certainly helped her fit in. The guys recognized her qualities and quickly made her a part of the team.

In fact, they accepted her so well that George Stanley had to run interference so she would not be the brunt of too many practical jokes like the ones they played on each other. It was a mark of acceptance when you were the victim of a joke, and they sure relished in their attempts to play some on Claire.

She remembered one incident in particular. Everyone on the

force knew she was Irish and that her ancestors came from a seaside town on the St. George's Channel, Dungarvan, which they helped to found.   She was proud of her heritage and talked longingly of her desire to go and visit her family's namesake one day. She had not had the opportunity yet, but as a substitute, she celebrated St. Patrick's Day in earnest every year.

Claire would dress up in her gaudiest green clothing, plastered with Irish buttons and jewelry, on that special day. The other detectives loved to rib her about being so fanatical, but they didn't mind going out with her to celebrate after work at one of the Irish pubs. *No, they enjoyed tipping a few no matter the occasion!*

On one such outing they were savoring some green beer when a leprechaun came up to her and started dancing around the table. All the guys had silly smiles on their faces, Claire would realize later, but at the time she just thought he was part of the scenery.

Oh yeah, he was part of the 'scenery' alright, and he made quite a 'scene' when he started to strip!

She couldn't believe her eyes when the so-called leprechaun paraded himself in front of her wearing only bikini underwear emblazoned with shamrocks.

He presented her with a real four-leaf clover while her buddies at the table laughed until tears rolled down their cheeks.

The guy was built like a Chippendale dancer and Claire had to admit that he looked pretty sexy in his Irish underwear.

She graciously accepted the 'souvenir' and gave the hunky leprechaun a big kiss in front of the other detectives just to show them she knew how to 'play the game' too.

Someone took a picture of her with the scantily clad leprechaun and hung it up on the bulletin board in the break room at work.

She never forgot that practical joke, and neither did her co-workers.

Chief was in on that one, she acknowledged. *He was at the table and was laughing so hard he almost fell off his chair.*

She found out later that he was the one who arranged the whole thing.

I'll put it down to remind people that he could be protective, but he could have fun too, she thought, as she tapped away on the computer.

And, she added, *he gave me a bouquet of yellow roses the next day. He knew they were my favorite, and he wanted to make sure I wasn't mad at him.*

Of course, I wasn't mad! It was funny, funny enough to become part of the post's folklore, a story everyone loved to tell year after year.

He gave me roses for my retirement party too, she remembered, *and they're still beautiful, sitting in a vase on the dining room table.*

She hesitated, considering an idea that had just popped into her head.

Hmmm, maybe I'll present him with some roses after my talk...or, better yet, give them to Mary as a token of my sympathy for having to put up with him during retirement!

Claire chuckled as she thought about how difficult it would be for Chief to settle down and not have the day-to-day operations of the state police to keep his mind occupied.

Mary will be a wreck! He doesn't have that many hobbies and you can only do so much fishing.

Oh well, she decided, *it will be a learning process for both of them, and I'm sure they can handle it.*

I'm handling it pretty well, she decided.

Just wish I could find out why these things keep appearing in my yard...and why I think they have something to do with Libby Newman.

Claire shook her head and forced herself to stop thinking about it, and get back to her speechwriting.

But when she completed the tribute, she found herself staring at the folder containing the information from the Libby Newman case again.

Knowing that something was gnawing at her, she shrugged her shoulders and opened the file, realizing that she wouldn't be able to concentrate on anything else until she investigated it further.

She was drawn to the information that included the identification of the victim and the search for the woman.

Claire read the physical description through, noting that Libby was of slender build, five feet, four inches tall, long blond hair, blue eyes, pretty by any standards.

Identifying marks?   Yes, she remembered, *there was an identifying mark. She had a tattoo on her right ankle.*

Her mother had mentioned that during the interview. She never liked that Libby had a tattoo, even though it was tastefully done and in a discreet location, not noticeable to most people.

Now let me see, Claire thought, *what was that tattoo anyway?*

She read through the report and gasped when she came upon the information she was looking for.

A rose! Libby had a rose tattoo on her ankle!

But that's not so strange, Claire reasoned. *Lots of people have a rose tattoo, especially women. It's one of the most common according to tattoo artists.* She remembered talking to one of them about it when she was investigating the case.

So, why should it surprise me that it was a rose tattoo when I was just thinking about roses?

"It's just a coincidence. What do they call that? Synchronism. Yeah, that's it. I'm having a synchronistic moment."

Laughing, Claire shook her head, bent down, and tried to return to her reading.

My mind was on roses and that's why it jumped out at me in the report, nothing more, she told herself.

Adding, *but the coincidences between this case and my present-day life are piling up, and it's hard not to recognize that fact!*

She attempted to concentrate on the report once again as she read through the search summary.

Libby was reported missing the next day by someone at Glenco. She had not come to work that morning and she always called in.

She used a relay operator to call and everyone in the office was familiar with the procedure and how to take a message.

One of the staff in personnel called Libby's home through the operator and did not get an answer. They waited quite some time before hanging up. Both knew you needed to give a deaf person time to see the flashing light and answer the phone, but after twenty rings, they suspended their efforts.

They tried calling an hour later thinking Libby might have overslept. This sequence was repeated throughout the day with no luck.

When the relay operator and staff failed to reach Libby, the employee in the personnel office expressed her concerns to the office manager, Ron Adams. He knew where she lived because he had taken her home a few times and he agreed to stop there on his way home.

"That's where we came in," Claire whispered to herself.

When Mr. Adams could not get an answer by ringing the doorbell, he decided to check further.

Libby had an alarm hooked up to the front door so when someone pushed the doorbell, flashing lights would alert her that someone was at the door.

He observed that the front porch light was still on, like someone had left it on from the night before.

He also noted the front door was unlocked, so he went in and looked around.

He saw nothing out of the ordinary but was bothered by the fact that Libby's purse was on the dining room table. He sensed that she would have taken it with her if she had gone anywhere.

He also knew that she usually kept her door locked, even before the divorce, because she never felt completely safe living out in the country alone.

He checked the garage. Her car was still parked there, further alarming him.

Altogether this concerned him enough to call the sheriff from his cell phone and report her missing.

Sheriff Carson, in turn, called us when he realized it might involve a wider search area, Claire remembered.

Ron Adams also gave the name and phone number of Libby's mother, which he had found next to her phone.

When we called her, Claire remembered, *she was concerned too.* She had seen Libby the day before when she stopped by her mom's house for a surprise visit.

Libby left around 6:00 p.m. and did not seem distressed or sick at the time. She told her mother she was going home to have supper and watch some television. Nothing out of the ordinary, nothing indicating she was in danger.

Or, maybe she was planning something and didn't want her mother to know?

That was the question no one could answer except Libby, and she hadn't been around to let anyone know what really happened...not in the last four years...not since she vanished.

CHAPTER SEVEN

The next day Claire spent most of her time fine-tuning the speech and getting ready for the retirement dinner. She checked outside earlier in the morning and was relieved to see that nothing new appeared in the snow, but she chose to leave the blood and shoeprints there in case she decided to call Jim Hoppes and have him take a look at it. She had not had the time to do that since then, but made a mental note to call him first thing the next morning, providing the mystery had not been resolved by then.

There has to be a logical explanation, she thought. *I don't want to discuss it with the guys tonight, even though they might be able to shed some light on the whole matter.*

She grinned. *They would tease me unmercifully if they knew how I was connecting it to the Libby Newman case.*

No, best to keep it to myself, Claire decided.

But, she couldn't help thinking about Libby. *Such an innocent victim!*

During the investigation, Libby's friends and family painted a picture of a pretty, sweet young woman who was trying to do something with her life in spite of her deafness.

It sounded like she had a lot of the same characteristics as a young Claire Dungarvan. She was ambitious, stubborn, determined to make the most out of her life.

When Libby finally found love, she embraced it with all her heart, giving in to the one weakness she possessed—her desire to be loved by another and have the kind of lifestyle she had always dreamt about. She wanted the husband, family, and home-- everything women are groomed to expect from an early age.

Unfortunately that dream dissolved quickly, and it must have been heartbreaking for her to experience.

Some members in her family had a hunch that she wasn't happy, even though her pride would have kept her from sharing it, and her lifelong habit of not sharing her innermost feelings with anyone could have played a role in her unwillingness to inform them.

"And that's why I can't get her out of my mind. She reminds me so much of myself."

Tears started to form in Claire's eyes but she quickly swiped them away. She thought back to Doug Walling, her first love and a fellow state trooper at the time.

She bowed her head in sadness when she remembered the night he was killed three years ago.

He had been issuing a speeding ticket out on the interstate. No one, except people in law enforcement maybe, could imagine how treacherous it would be to stand beside a car, checking license and insurance information. Police officers do it all the time, but it is particularly dangerous when out on the interstate.

As Doug stepped back from the speeder's car and shone his flashlight on the papers in his hand, a truck came careening out of nowhere.

The driver hit Doug so hard that it threw his body up into the air, landing twenty feet away.

When Claire arrived, the paramedics told her there was nothing they could do; he was already gone. The driver who caused the accident never stopped. The speeder was in shock and couldn't offer any help. Since it happened in the middle of the night, no witnesses were close enough to observe any distinguishing characteristics about the truck, just that it was a semi. And, unfortunately, Doug's in-car video camera was not working at the time of the accident.

Officers did a thorough investigation of truckers in the area, but the driver was never found. If he had reported damage to his truck, no company reported it to the police.

Claire was so overcome with grief that she had to take a week off from work. *No, to be honest, Marvin and George ordered me to take the week off!*

She attended the funeral but it was one of the hardest things she ever had to do.

Doug's parents were especially distraught. He was their youngest son and the only one to follow in his father's footsteps.

Herb Walling had been a sheriff's deputy in Jenson County, just south of Indianapolis, for twenty years.

The one positive outcome was that the Indiana state legislature put a new law into effect that made it mandatory for drivers on the interstate to move over into the middle lane when passing a site where an emergency vehicle was parked or a patrol officer had a car pulled over on the shoulder. Since then, the number of fatalities had decreased significantly.

"Too late to help Doug though."

Claire thought back to all the regrets she felt after the tragedy.

He wanted the same things Libby Newman wanted—loving spouse, home, family—and neither had the opportunity to fulfill their dreams.

If I hadn't been so selfish! Claire balled up her hand into a fist.

Adding sadly, *but I knew what I wanted too, and it was my career.*

During the investigation into Libby's disappearance, Claire found herself going over the same information, same search areas, same interviews, just trying to find some piece of evidence that hadn't stood out before, something that might lead her to the truth about what happened.

But, when Doug died, and after two years of following lead after lead that eventually led nowhere, she put Libby's folder in the cold case file where it had languished ever since. She never forgot it, but she stopped thinking about it all the time…until now. Now it was coming back, consuming her life, almost to the extent that you might say it was haunting her.

CHAPTER EIGHT

Claire checked her image in the mirror and was satisfied with what she saw staring back at her. "Not bad for an old broad of 55," she joked.

It helped to boost her ego, but the primary motivation behind the remark was to eradicate any worrisome memories and enjoy the evening at hand.

The retirement party would give her an opportunity to see friends, laugh, honor her beloved 'Chief', and relish the moment with him.

"And, get my mind on other things!"

She grabbed her coat and headed downstairs.

Turning the light on in the garage, she peered inside before remembering she had left her car in the driveway after running to the floral shop to pick up the roses.

She playfully smacked her forehead with the heel of her hand and smiled as she went out the back door, locked it, and walked to the car.

Claire was in a good mood as she thought about seeing her friends at the dinner. But she couldn't put the day's happenings behind her and therefore couldn't resist looking up towards the front yard. Even though she didn't really expect to see anything, it had become a habit, she admitted, *almost an obsession*.

Glancing quickly, she had her hand on the car door when she realized she had seen something new!

"Not again," she groaned.

Claire fought with herself to open the door and drive to the party without a second thought, but she lost the battle. She let go of the handle and reluctantly turned to get a closer look at what she had seen in the snow.

Trudging up the hill, she thought, *why am I doing this to myself?*

As she edged nearer, squinting to make out the burst of color in the otherwise glaring white snow, Claire saw...*red...more blood?*

"No, it has a distinctive shape," she whispered.

She analyzed the outline, still walking towards it. *Long, slender, at one end...that part is darker in color...splash of red at the top.*

Making her way closer and closer, Claire suddenly stopped dead in her tracks.

A red rose! What would a rose be doing in the yard at this time of the year?

She picked it up and studied it carefully. *Not stiff or frozen from the cold. The color of the bloom is still bright and the petals are firm to the touch, not limp like they would be if it had been outside in the frigid air for a while.*

She glanced around, looking both ways on the road, to check and see if someone was nearby.

No one! You would think that I would see the person who left it. It's too fresh to have been here that long.

Round and round, Claire twisted it in her hand like the questions twirling inside her head.

Hmmm...coincidences seem to be piling up. I'm taking roses to the party tonight. That started me thinking about Libby's rose tattoo. What, if anything, does it all mean?

Dumfounded, Claire made her way back to the car, still holding the rose. *This is crazy! I have to stop thinking about her!*

She tossed it in the back seat and turned the key in the ignition, proclaiming as she backed out of the driveway, "Not going to let anything spoil the party!"

CHAPTER NINE

The parking lot of the restaurant was filled with law enforcement vehicles from all over the state.

Chief's personal car was parked under the canopy at the front door, gaily decorated with streamers and signs on the windshields. Claire saw Jim Hoppes attaching an envelope to the wipers and waved to him as she pulled into a parking space.

He waited for her to exit the car and called out, "Hey, Claire. Looks like you finally have your opportunity to get even with him for all the years of teasing he put you through!"

She hurried to join up with him, responding as she walked, "Yeah and I'll make him pay!"

Jim laughed as they turned to go into Hollyfield restaurant together.

"I'm so glad to see you tonight!"

He looks great! Can't believe he's not married! I think I remember something about him being married before but that was a long time ago. I guess he hasn't found anyone else. Sounds like someone I know--myself. Claire smiled at the thought and made a hasty decision.

"I wanted to talk to you about something. Do you think we could sit together?" They stood at the doorway of the banquet room. Claire looked around, scouting for an empty table.

Smiling, Jim replied, "Sure, no problem...I'd never turn down an offer like that."

Bright blue eyes took in Claire, making her heart leap. She couldn't help but notice how handsome he was. *Blond hair, just a touch of white around the temples beginning to show, dimples when he smiles, a little over six feet tall, broad shoulders, strong athletic body, kept in shape; I like that!*

Several people came up to say hello and Chief waved to them, blowing her a kiss from the dais set up in front. Mary was sitting next to him and motioned for her to come up. She asked Jim to find them some seats and went to pay her respects to the guests of honor.

"Mary, I don't know how you've managed to put up with him all these years."

She handed her the yellow roses and continued, "By the way, these are for you."

Captain Hennessey stood and hugged Claire, planting a kiss on her cheek. "Smart move, lady."

"Oh, Claire, they're beautiful!" Mary exclaimed. "Thank you so much!" She admired the flowers, tears welling up in her eyes.

"Here," she patted the seat next to her, "sit and tell us what you've been doing since your retirement."

"Not a whole lot," Claire replied, while taking a seat, "and that's the way I like it."

"By the way, I'm writing, working on a novel," she continued.

"That's wonderful! What's it about?"

"Well, it's about a case I worked on a few years ago."

"Let me guess," Chief interrupted, "the Libby Newman case, right?"

"You guessed it, Marvin."

She hesitated and then said, "I'm having a difficult time with it though. It seems to be invading my life right now."

Claire smiled uneasily and peered out at the crowd. She saw Jim motioning to join him at the table because the waiters were beginning to bring in the food. "I see they're about ready to start serving. I'd better get to my table."

When she stood up, Chief hugged her one more time and looked into her eyes, "You know you shouldn't take your work home with you, especially when you're retired.

He continued to hold onto her, staring, "Call me if you need some help."

She nodded her head up and down slowly and gave his hand a squeeze as she turned to leave. "I will."

Maybe I'll do just that, she thought, walking across the room.

"So, how's he holding up?" Jim held Claire's chair for her.

"Ornery as ever," she responded. "Mary is the one who has my sympathy though. Marvin is not one to sit around and do nothing. He'll miss the mental challenges of the job, if nothing else."

"Yeah, you're probably right. But, maybe he'll surprise us and find a stimulating hobby."

He added, "By the way, what are you doing with all your free time?"

Jim took a sip of water while waiting for Claire to answer.

She paused as if making a decision and finally said, "Well, I'm glad you asked because I wanted to talk to you about something..."

"Claire, so nice to see you again! Oh, hi, Jim, good to see you too, but you're not as pretty to look at as she is."

Jim looked up to see George Stanley standing by the table.

He laughed, "I agree with you on both counts, George."

He stood and shook hands with Claire's former supervisor, inviting him to join them at the table.

Wondering what it was she wanted to discuss with him, he silently pledged to make time later in the evening for the two of them to talk.

For her part, Claire joined the conversation, even appearing relieved to have the interruption.

Might be best if I wait to talk to Jim. I'm not sure if having so much free time has caused my imagination to go haywire!

She paused, *but if I see anything else in the snow, I'm calling him!*

The rest of the night went by quickly. Claire's speech drew many laughs, sparking memories and conversations around the room.

On her way back to the table, she was stopped by former co-workers for handshakes and hugs. And, by the time she approached their table, she noticed that Jim was gone.

The waiter was cleaning and she asked him if he had seen the man who had been sitting with her.

He shook his head 'no' and continued clearing away the plates and silverware.

Why would he leave and not tell me?

Feeling hurt and disappointed, Claire gathered her things and prepared to leave the banquet hall.

But I did decide to wait before I involve someone else, she remembered. *I'm not even sure what I'd tell him at this point!*

She shrugged her shoulders and walked out to the car.

Back inside the waiter continued to clean the table. He didn't notice that one of the napkins had writing on it. He wadded up all the paper goods and threw them in the trash bag.

CHAPTER TEN

The next morning Claire was having breakfast when the phone rang.

"Did you get my message?"

"No, I wondered where you went! What happened? What message?"

Jim sighed, "I'm sorry, Claire. I got a phone call from dispatch and they needed me at the Conservancy. We had a pretty bad accident right out in front of the clubhouse and they called for me. I left a message on a napkin because I didn't have any paper to write on."

"I guess the waiter must have thrown it away," he continued.

Claire smiled, "Not a problem. I thought maybe you didn't like my company."

"Now, you know that's not true! I am so glad you asked me to sit with you. I'd been meaning to stop by and see you."

"In fact," he added, "I was wondering if I could come over today and we could have that talk?"

A long silence ensued. *Now what do I do! Should I tell him?*

Finally, "Hold on, Jim. I need to see who's at the door."

Hope he buys that, she thought as she went to the front door. Her intention was to look and see if anything else had shown up in the yard.

Jim heard a small scream through the phone line and then eerie quiet.

"Claire!" Silence. Then, he heard footsteps coming closer.

"Claire, is that you?"

"I think you'd better come over now," she said as she hung up the phone.

Claire stood next to Jim as he bent over to investigate what she had seen earlier that morning.

"Why would someone leave a knife in your yard?"

The question floated in the air. Claire shrugged her shoulders indecisively.

"Now, you're sure it wasn't here yesterday, right?"

She nodded her head in agreement.

"And," he added, "the blood was the first thing to show up, then the prints, and more blood yesterday?"

"Yes, I saw the blood for the first time day before yesterday and then the shoeprints, and more blood."

Jim stood there quietly assessing the situation, trying to come up with a logical explanation.

Claire cleared her throat, "And then there was the rose..."

"What rose?" He looked at her suspiciously.

She motioned for him to follow her down to the driveway. Opening the car door, she grabbed the flower out of the backseat. It was a beautiful long-stemmed red rose. "I found it in the yard yesterday before I left for the party. And, I brought it with me to show you but you left..."

Jim interrupted her, "You found it in the yard too? Same place?"

"Yes, same place, fresh as it is now, no frost, no wilting."

"Hmm, that is strange."

He held the flower, fingering the petals, mesmerized by its survival in the snow with the accompanying cold weather.

Then he looked at Claire and said, "I thought it might be a hunter until you mentioned the rose. Now, I don't know what to think." He continued to stare at it, lost in thought, striving to come up with an answer to the mystery.

"You have any ideas on what it might mean?"

"Actually I might have something, but it's pretty farfetched."

She hesitated and then asked, "Would you have time for a cup of coffee? It might take a while to explain."

"Just let me grab that knife, radio in so they know where I'm at, and I'll join you inside in a few minutes."

He ran up the hill, still clutching the single red rose, and Claire went into the house.

Jim sipped his coffee carefully, allowing the hot liquid enough time to coat his throat and leave a warm feeling in his chest. He also made use of the time to gather his thoughts and try to comprehend what Claire had just told him.

He remembered the case—*young deaf woman, disappeared one night, never seen or heard from again. He knew the police had questioned her ex-husband but he had a solid alibi.*

And now Claire tells me that the items in the snow might be related to that case!

"Do you think someone is trying to scare you into not writing about it?"

Claire cleared her throat and paused before answering, "Could be, or I wonder if someone is trying to help me solve the case."

Jim stared at her, letting this sink in. "The only people who could do that are the victim...and the perpetrator...if someone did cause harm to her. You don't know if she is dead or alive, do you?"

She looked down at her coffee cup, "I have my suspicions."

"Well, come on, you need to open up if I'm going to help. What are you thinking?"

Sighing, "It sounds crazy but ...."

"Listen, Claire, you and I have been in law enforcement long enough to know that strange things do happen..."

She put up her hand, interrupting him, "You're right. Let me pour us both another cup and I'll tell you what's on my mind."

Jim watched her as she filled his cup to the brim, but she didn't return his gaze. Claire seemed miles away, but as she sat back down, she quickly and efficiently began to share what she thought had happened to Libby Newman.

Chapter Eleven

In bed that night, Claire couldn't sleep. Shadows danced on the walls, remnants of an almost full moon streaming through the window. She let her imagination play off the shapes as she thought back to what she and Jim had discussed that morning.

Could she be dead? Seems like a long time for someone to just disappear without a trace.

Claire stared at one particularly menacing outline on the opposite wall.

Interesting....Jim thinks her husband had something to do with her disappearance... and he's the one scaring me by putting the signs in the snow!

But why would he do that? Did he kill her? Is he taunting me? Is this a game to him?

She tossed her head back and forth on the pillow. *I just don't believe he would be that stupid!*

After all, if he did kill her, he's gotten away with murder for four years now and wouldn't want to bring attention back to the case.

But if it's not him, who else?

Gradually, sleep overcame Claire, and she was no longer aware of the shadows. Composed by moonlight, they scattered around the room...unlike the one that settled into her dream. It stood firm and soon took on a reality of its own. Mist became substance; features sharpened and became visible, and a yielding, feminine form evolved. A soft mewing sound escaped her lips as the dream-state apparition became recognizable to Claire. Libby Newman was ready to tell her story.

A tangle of bed sheets served as evidence of a night spent turning and tossing. Claire rubbed her eyes and tried to disengage from the material wrapped around her legs and arms. Kicking and flailing, she finally managed to free her body. But before crawling out of bed, she stared at the ceiling and walls, remembering her dream.

Dazed, she recalled, *unless I'm crazy, Libby appeared to me in my dream last night!*

But, can that be?

She folded back the last bit of sheet and blanket and swung around to sit up, saying aloud, "It must have been my imagination."

Claire climbed out of bed and made her way to the bathroom, as more flashbacks from the dream came flooding in.

She rubbed her eyes and tried to erase the fogginess in her head as she walked down the hallway. Not paying attention to where she was going, Claire stumbled and stubbed her big toe on the door frame. Wincing in pain, she grabbed the sink and stood there for a minute, trying to regain strength—and sanity.

This is ridiculous! Now I'm having... nightmares! Worse yet, I'm letting them get to me.

"I need a cup of coffee," she mumbled, staring in the mirror, frowning at the tousled hair and sleepy eyes she saw reflected in the glass.

The telephone rang as she tried to shake the last vestiges of pain emanating from her toe and the first telltale poundings of a headache. She placed her fingers up to her temples in a futile attempt to rub away the dull ache before she had to succumb to the relief of a couple of aspirin with her coffee.

Recovering as much as she could, she quickly walked to the kitchen, hurrying to pick up the phone after the third ring.

"Hello."

"Hope I didn't wake you."

Claire smiled and clutched the phone tighter at the familiar sound of Jim's voice, the aches and pains fading into oblivion.

"No, I was just getting ready to fix some coffee." And, quickly, without hesitation, she asked, "Want to come over and have some breakfast with me?"

"Seems like this is becoming a regular routine," Jim responded teasingly.

"Not yet, but who knows what the future might hold."

She grimaced after she said it, while a blush started to spread across her face.

"Hey, I like the sound of that!" Pausing, he continued, "And, I have some ideas I want to share with you. Would you mind?"

"Of course not, I have something I need to tell you too," she replied.

"I'm on my way."

Staring at the receiver, she heard the click of the phone on the other end. She couldn't move or even breathe for several seconds. Claire realized that she couldn't back down now. She had to tell him about her dream. Carefully, she placed the phone in its cradle and waited for Jim to arrive.

"I know it was her," Claire sighed, "and you can think what you want, but it was Libby Newman and she was trying to tell me something." She clenched her jaw and waited for him to object.

Silence stretched seconds into minutes. Jim swirled his fork around in circles, carefully picking up the last bite of his egg. He observed it as if he were deciding to eat the bite or leave it. Finally he put the fork down on the plate, with the egg still on it, and stared at Claire for what seemed like a long time.

"Okay, tell me exactly what she did. Try to remember every detail of the dream," he encouraged her.

"She...she stood there just looking at me. Her expression was so sad. It was like she wanted to tell me something but didn't know how."

Deep in thought, Claire stopped for a minute and then a rush of words came pouring out. "She showed me some pictures...a place, close to the water...there were trees all around. You have to walk through the woods to get there. I felt as if this was where she is."

Pausing, Claire felt a tear start to form in the corner of her eye. "I'm not sure if she's dead, but she wants someone to know what happened and where she's located."

She picked up her coffee cup, draining the last few drops, and grimaced at the bitter taste before continuing with her story.

"Libby kept doing the same gesture, over and over again...but I couldn't understand it!" Claire clutched her coffee cup so tightly that her knuckles turned white.

Jim reached over and placed his hand on top of hers. "Tell me what it looked like. Can you show me?"

Gently removing her hands from his grasp, she placed her cup on the table, looked at her hands, and slowly began to form the sign she remembered Libby using. Awkwardly at first, shaping her hands much like a baby speaking his first word, fashioning and making it his own, Claire began to form the gesture she remembered in her dream. She uncurled her left hand and laid it flat, fingers together, palm up. With her right hand, she formed a fist and placed it squarely in the middle of her left hand. Then she lifted them up together, the outstretched hand supporting the fist.

"Like this, I think," she said.

Jim studiously watched her. He thought he knew what the sign meant but he wanted to be sure.

"This?" He formed the fist and placed it on top of his open hand.

"Yes, that's exactly what it looked like!"

"Do you know what it means?" she asked excitedly.

"I think so."

He plunged ahead, "If I remember my sign language correctly, she was saying 'help'. I took a beginning class in American Sign Language a few years ago when we had some Deaf residents move into the Conservancy and I think that's what it means."

He added, "I have my book at home. If you want, I can bring it over for you to look at."

"So, you believe me, Jim?"

"Of course I believe you, Claire. You're too level-headed to be making this up."

He paused and shook his head, "Though it is hard to imagine…why a person would want to communicate through a dream. Why didn't she contact you by phone or letter?" His voice trailed off before he could finish.

"If she's still alive," Claire added, as if reading his thoughts.

He leaned over, rested his elbows on the table, and placed his hands on the sides of his face, rubbing them up and down across his cheeks.

Finally he sighed, raised his eyes to meet hers, and said, "Well, where do we start?"

Claire smiled and patted his cheek affectionately. "Thanks for believing in me. It means a lot just to have your offer of help, but I probably need to gather more information before I do anything else."

"Alright, I'll bring you my sign language book this afternoon. You might need it in case she tries to send you any more messages…and I'm sure she will," he quickly added.

Then, Jim shared his ideas with her, "I'll take the knife down to Nashtown and see if we can find any fingerprints on it. I'd like to get a sample of the blood too. Need to find out if it is human or animal."

"You keep the rose in a safe place; see if it begins to lose some of its freshness…or if it continues to look the same as it does now…and check your yard for any more clues."

"Also, write down any information you get from your dreams. I think she'll probably try to contact you again, especially if she knows we are aware of the message she's sending us."

A car flashed by, just skirting his peripheral vision enough to cause Trent Newman to swerve back into his lane. The other driver gave him the 'universal hand gesture' as he maneuvered his car in front of Trent's truck. He didn't bother to reciprocate the 'favor' since he realized that he had been close to falling asleep behind the wheel and might have caused an accident if he hadn't been startled by the car's proximity.

Grabbing for some gum in the glove compartment, he tried to shake the cobwebs from his brain as he unwrapped a piece for himself. Chewing something helped stimulate his senses while he focused on the road ahead and thought about the last week and the reason for his lack of sleep.

The visions...why did they start now? It's been four years and...nothing.

He slammed his fist down on the steering wheel, hoping to eradicate the anger swelling up inside him like a boiling pot of hot grease. It threatened to spill over and become an uncontrollable fury if he didn't take steps to repress it. Subconsciously, he chewed his gum harder, absorbing the flavor until it almost disappeared. Road rage was manageable to him; this was not.

He grabbed the wheel with such intensity that his hand clenched tautly and he lost feeling in his fingers. Unaware of the tingling sensation, he forged ahead, determined to make his deadline. But his mind began to wander—back to the dreams.

The first time she appeared to him, Trent was so shocked that he woke up suddenly and could feel himself shaking violently, causing him to break out in a cold sweat. It happened so quickly that he later speculated he might be imagining it.

Imagining it in my dream? I don't think so! It was Libby and she was trying to tell me something!

He lifted his hand to massage his forehead and felt the dead weight of his fingers as they caressed the worry lines forming above his eyes. Shaking his hand to bring blood flow back into his fingers, he remembered the next time she appeared to him.

It felt like my head hadn't even hit the pillow that next night, he remembered, *when she invaded my dreams again.*

"Nightmares were more like it," he said aloud.

Swirling in, out, and around, Libby wove a tapestry of images that Trent would not soon forget. Her fingers and hands flew. Scenes flitted about like butterflies attracted to a flower.

She was sending me a message!

Even though he couldn't understand all the signs she was using, he knew she would be back—time and time again—until she was sure the message had been received. Her intent was clear. Communication was not the only objective. She wanted to ensure her killer was caught.

CHAPTER TWELVE

Preoccupied with thoughts of signs in the snow, Claire did not hear the solid rap on the front door until it became a persistent, urgent knocking that could not be ignored.

Carefully folding her dishtowel on the countertop, she turned around to see Myra peering in through the montage of flowers on the wreath hanging over the center pane of glass.

Claire waved and hastened over to let her in.

"Have you looked outside today?"

Myra rushed ahead, not waiting for an answer. "I hope you were able to talk to Jim. Unfortunately there's not much left."

She shook her head disappointedly. "The water's pretty much washed everything away."

As Myra motioned for her to come outside, Claire looked at her quizzically. "Whatever are you talking about, Myra?"

"She's talking about the water bubbling up out here in the yard." Claire looked up to see Kate standing next to a small pond of water seeping out of the ground.

"Good Lord! What in the world is that?" Claire hurried over to get a closer look at the liquid oozing forth from the area where the shoe prints and the blood had been yesterday.

All three women stood transfixed, not talking, but trying to make sense out of the whole scenario.

Finally Myra spoke, "Kate and I were just beginning our morning walk when I glanced over and noticed water coming up in your yard. I thought it might have been the same spot where you showed me the blood and prints, so I came in for a closer look."

"Do you think you might have a water leak?" Kate stared while Claire knelt down to touch the fluid.

Shaking her hand of the drops that accumulated there, Claire seemed puzzled as she replied, "That's strange. The water is fairly warm…and there's no freezing as it comes up through the ground."

The three of them quietly studied the unusual anomaly for several minutes.

"Well, I'm glad Jim saw the evidence and was able to take some samples before they were washed away."

Claire's head jerked up when she realized that Jim had only left a short while ago. "At least I think he did," she whispered.

The two other women didn't quite understand what Claire was talking about, but noticed her concern and rushed to reassure her.

"Don't worry about it, Claire," Kate said. "It's probably just a coincidence that the water is here."

Myra jumped in, "You might want to call the office and have the guys come over and check it."

Helpfully, "Maybe you have a leak. It's close to the meter pit," she added.

Claire thanked the ladies and wished them well as they started their walk.

Yeah, like that's going to make me feel better! Just what I don't need right now—a water leak! She smiled as she thought about their futile attempts to make her feel better.

But her smile turned to a frown when she considered the latest clue. *Because that's what I think it is—a clue, not a water leak. The water is warm and why would it just spring up like that?*

"I need to call Jim," she spoke aloud while walking back to the house.

Worried, she hoped he was able to take some samples. *But, what if he wasn't?*

Black spread over the landscape at a maddeningly slow pace. Ominous clouds loomed overhead, signaling the coming winter storm…and a figure watched from the woods, waiting patiently.

But fingers drummed silently against a leg and hands flew out from a body in response to growing tension…and the wait continued, with the sentinel desiring the secret that could give an answer to what happened to Libby Newman.

Murkiness finally swept away illumination and the lone form crept slowly towards the house, so quietly that the steps emitted no sounds, no crunching, no twigs snapping, only the hush of falling snow on top of an established wintry foundation, already laid out, blending the old with the new.

The shape appeared in front of Libby's house quickly; even the small creatures in the woods would have startled if they had been present to note the arrival.

Focused on the goal but mindful of any intrusion, slowly, stealthily, it moved towards the garage, keeping surroundings always in focus so as not to ignore any signs of another's nearness.

A side door that allowed access to the garage was the destination, and it loomed larger as the silent figure approached.

Then, the door knob rattled ever so slightly and a smile lit up dim countenance.

It's unlocked!

A faint swish of air and the figure disappeared. Could it have been a sigh of relief coming from someone? Or, could it have been the sound of a door opening to allow the shadowy trespasser access to the secret?

Time might tell but the brooding storm erupted into a fury of foreboding, unleashing darkness that hid the answer from all but one.

Jim Hoppes studied the impending storm as he stood outside the new Law Enforcement facility in Nashtown, Indiana. A frown formed, but it was hard to tell if it was in response to the promise of several new inches of snow, or because of the information he had just received.

The sheriff had been very agreeable to Jim's request to use the lab to check the blood samples and knife he had brought in. Maybe he was eager to show off the new technology they had, or maybe he was just in a good mood. Either way, Jim was grateful for the help.

The frown changed to a smile when he remembered the way Sheriff Wayne proudly offered him a tour of the new building while the lab technician poured over the blood and knife.

"Best jail in southern Indiana, Jim. Bar none."

"I agree, Ken, but you sure had to jump through some hoops to get it, didn't you."

Sheriff Wayne shook his head, "True, true, but I think the taxpayers are coming around," he paused, "Especially now that they see how much it's contributing to the community."

Jim laughed, "You mean now that you have more room to put the bad guys behind bars instead of walking the streets of downtown Nashtown, don't you."

Ken smiled, "You wouldn't be making fun of our little town, would you, Jim?"

Both men chuckled, remembering the long drawn-out struggles with the County Council over the expenditure of a new jail. Tempers flared, but in the long run, both sides had agreed that it would bring new revenues to the county and a safer environment for Nashtown.

As they stood in the lobby, looking around the facility, the door to the lab opened.

The county's only technician, Shirley Trusty, stood facing both men with hands on her hips. Her hair had a patch on the right side where tufts flailed out uncontrollably.

Almost like she'd been scratching her head, Jim thought.

"Are you ready to hear my conclusions?"

She motioned for them to come in without waiting for an answer, and closed the door behind them.

A few flakes of new snow started to fall on Jim's face as he stood outside the jail, still lost in thought.

What does it all mean? And, more importantly, how am I going to tell Claire?

He was having a hard time understanding the ramifications of what Shirley had just told him and Sheriff Wayne.

After the results of the tests were given, they both went to Ken's office to discuss them further.

Jim explained where the blood samples came from and what had happened up to this point, leaving out any suspicions that they had about Libby.

Both men sat in silence, considering the possibilities, until Jim added, "I suppose this means you will need to get involved, right?"

The sheriff sat slumped in his chair, but immediately sat upright, putting his feet squarely on the floor in front of him and giving credence to his large stature, all six feet, four inches and two hundred and twenty pounds of mostly muscle. Taking on the position of sheriff had not turned his body to fat like some of his predecessors had had happen to them.

"Of course you know what this means! It's either someone's idea of a sick joke or it's a deliberate threat to Claire! I tend to believe it's a threat."

Jim sat quietly before he calmly answered, "I know, Ken, but," he paused, gathering his thoughts and anticipating the angry barrage that might follow, "could you at least give us a few days to investigate this on our own?"

He rushed ahead before the sheriff had any time to lash out. "You know Claire. She's a good detective. She's got some ideas about what might have happened and she's asked for my help. Would you let the two of us look into this before you get any of your men involved?"

Ken Wayne stared at Jim and opened his mouth, then shut it again, allowing precious seconds to tick by on the clock. He lowered his head and shuffled some papers on his desk before answering, "Okay, it's your jurisdiction anyway," he sighed.

"But," he looked up at Jim with fire in his eyes, "you'd better get back to me with some news no later than Friday."

Jim extended his hand, and as the two men shook hands, the sheriff warned him again, "No later than Friday…I mean it."

Before letting Jim's hand go, he added, "Claire might be in for far more than you two can imagine."

Driving back to the Sweetwater Conservancy, Jim kept his eyes on the road, slowing down considerably when a sudden burst of snowflakes clouded his vision and made for almost whiteout conditions. Patches of new snow had already formed on the asphalt. Over packed-down existing ice, it caused treacherous road conditions.

The tires on this squad car aren't the best. Should have replaced those months ago...if the County had given the Conservancy their share of property tax revenues when they were supposed to!

Jim shook his head. *Need to take my mind off politics and keep an eye on other drivers. Can't predict how people will drive in this weather.*

Luckily not many drivers were on the roads. Brown County residents were used to what the snowy circumstances could do to their back roads.

Many had made their way to the local grocery store, stocked up with enough food to feed an army for weeks, and arrived home safely, ready to wait out the storm in confidence, knowing that they would be well-fed, warm and safe for the duration.

Chances are they had been listening to the radio when the weather forecast had come on to predict an additional seven inches of new snow before nightfall. That would have been enough to make all but the heartiest run for the security of home, well before quitting time.

With his mind on the weather, but also on the information he had to share with Claire, Jim recalled what Shirley had told them.

This changes the whole picture, he thought. *Even though it will take a few more days to get the full results, knowing what we now know about the blood is disturbing enough!*

Coming up on a slight curve in the road, Jim gently let up on the accelerator, adjusting the speed down to what he thought was safe enough to accommodate the weather conditions.

Unfortunately, as he felt the car begin to turn, he also felt the back tires slide dangerously close to the side of the road, and before he could bring it out, Jim looked up to see the fence and the tree beside it looming alarmingly close.

Before the car crashed into both, all he could think about was making sure Claire knew the danger she might be in…and then he blacked out.

CHAPTER THIRTEEN

"Why isn't he answering his phone?" Claire paced back and forth, taking time every few minutes to look out her window or check the weather forecast on TV.

At first she had tried his home phone, thinking he might have already returned from Nashtown without stopping by or calling.

Maybe he just dropped the evidence off and doesn't have anything to tell me yet.

Or, she thought, *he might be sleeping. After all this has been a rough few days for him too!*

Finally, she had given in to her anxiety and called the Conservancy Office to see if he was still on duty. Laura, the new part-time receptionist, had responded that 'Yes indeed Jim was still on duty and should be returning from Nashtown any time'. She had assured Claire that she would have him call her as soon as he arrived.

Claire waited until after five o'clock but her concern started to mount as she watched the weather unfold outside and listened to the dire forecast on television for the rest of the evening.

Calling his cell phone repeatedly now, she felt the beginnings of fear grip her stomach. Her breath caught in her throat as her imagination conjured up all kinds of scenarios. She exhaled loudly and purposefully worked at calming herself down.

This is silly! He's probably safe at home, not wanting to be bothered. More than likely he left the samples and they won't have the results ready until later.

The persistent jangling of the phone brought her out of her thoughts and made her jump.

She rushed to pick it up. "Hello," she answered urgently.

"Good. You're there. I was hoping you weren't out in this weather."

"Chief! Hi!"

Before she could continue with social pleasantries, he interrupted her, "Listen, I'm calling because I got a phone call just a few minutes ago from your sheriff, Ken Wayne. You know Ken, right?"

"Yes, I know him," Claire answered cautiously.

"Well, he doesn't have your number since you just moved down there and he's trying to get in touch with you."

"Is there anything wrong, Marvin?" Claire's voice took on an even more serious tone.

"I guess Jim Hoppes came to see him today…about a case the two of you are working on together."

He paused before adding, "What the hell is that all about, Claire? Jesus Christ! You're supposed to be retired!"

"Calm down, Chief," she cautioned him, "Just tell me what's going on with Jim. I've been trying to reach him and so far, nothing."

"He's been in an accident, Claire."

Her heart skipped a beat and her hand flew up to her mouth, "An accident! What happened? Is he alright?"

"He's going to be fine, but he's in the hospital."

"What hospital?"

"Frederick General," Chief responded, "but you're not going by yourself if you have any ideas about that. Wait there. I'm coming to pick you up."

He abruptly hung up before Claire could protest.

"Chief, are you insane?" Claire yelled in the phone but the only sound she heard in return was the dial tone, indicating he had already terminated the call.

"He shouldn't be driving down here in this weather!"

Claire dialed Chief's home phone number and Mary answered on the first ring.

"Has he left yet?"

"Of course," Mary responded, "do you think he would listen to me if he won't listen to you?"

Both women agreed that Marvin could be very stubborn, having shared many stories with each other about past incidents where he had been especially difficult at work… and at home!

Mary spoke up, "Don't worry, Claire. Jim will be okay. He's conscious and the reason Marvin wanted to take you there is because Jim has been asking for you and he didn't want you to come by yourself. Jim said he has something he needs to tell you right away."

"What did he want to tell me, Mary?"

"I'm not sure but Marvin said he kept saying that he had to warn you because the blood was human, whatever that meant."

Claire dropped the telephone on the floor.

"Claire, are you there? What happened? I heard a noise. Did you drop the phone?"

Picking it up gingerly, Claire took a deep breath, and quietly said, "I'm okay, Mary. I'll wait for Chief to get here."

"Are you sure you're okay?"

"I'm fine, Mary. You're right. I just dropped the telephone," she explained.

While looking out the patio door and keeping an eye on the driveway, she saw the headlights of a car turn onto the side road.

"Oh, gotta go. Marvin just arrived. Thanks for your help though, and you take care. I'll talk to you later."

Hanging up, Claire hurried to the closet, grabbed her coat, and ran downstairs as she heard the knocking at the back door.

Opening it, she saw the now retired Captain Hennessey standing there, attempting to brush the accumulating snowflakes off his shoulders, but with the rapidly falling precipitation, it was a lost cause.

"Chief," she admonished, "What were you thinking—coming out in this mess!"

His response was to reach out and hug her. With his hand resting gently on her elbow, he led her to the car, treading slowly through the clumps of snow left by the tire ruts in the driveway.

A lone figure stood watching as the car turned from the side road, lights shining on the steady, fine mist which was continuously gathering momentum. Fading into the distance, the headlights did not shine on the small batch of trees in the front yard. For if they had, the beams might have illuminated the form standing there, gazing at the house, sadness permeating its whole being.

But a sense of crisis would be present also. And by morning, the being would proclaim another sign— new drops of blood on a fresh blanket of snow.

CHAPTER FOURTEEN

Marvin and Claire sat in the lobby of Frederick General Hospital, waiting for the nurse to indicate that Jim was in a room and they could visit him.

When they had arrived at the hospital about an hour ago, the emergency room doctor explained that Jim had two cracked ribs, from the impact with the tree and the fence. He also had a deep cut on his forehead, which had required twelve stitches, but other than that, he was conscious, alert and would be transferred to a room so they could monitor him overnight.

Even though the cracked ribs were painful, Jim was feeling well enough to argue that he should be discharged. But the doctor was more insistent and eventually talked him into staying until morning. However, Jim asked that Claire be allowed to come to his room and visit with him for a few minutes.

He seemed especially anxious to tell her something and didn't want to be given any pain medication that might make him too drowsy, but he promised to take the pills once he had talked with Claire.

The doctor had not been happy with that part of the bargain, but asked the nurse to let him know when Claire arrived so he could discuss Jim's condition with her and they could start administering something for the pain.

Now Marvin and Claire were waiting for the nurse to tell them that Jim was in his room.

"Can you at least tell me why you're working when you should be retired and bored out of your mind, like me?" Chief looked at her with an exasperating grin on his face.

Claire smiled, glanced down the hallway for a few minutes like she was trying to decide if she should tell him or not.

She gazed back at him and said, "Okay, but you have to promise me that you'll listen to what I have to say before offering any opinions…and that you'll not get involved yourself."

Marvin sighed deeply and shrugged his shoulders, "My curiosity is getting the better of me," he paused, "but I reserve the right to offer assistance if I think I could help in any way…especially if you're involved."

Claire saw that he was not going to give in on that last part.

Unfortunately Chief had never sacrificed his 'big brother' role as far as she was concerned. He would always think of himself as her protector

Before Claire could open her mouth to respond, the nurse came up behind them and announced that Jim was in his room and she could see him now.

"Why don't you come with me, Chief? Between the two of us, Jim and I can fill you in on what has happened so far, and he can tell us both what he found out today."

Captain Hennessey nodded and they both stood up to follow the nurse.

In the darkness of the garage, a thin beam emanated from a flashlight, bobbing, as if searching for something. The light trailed up and down the walls, slowly at first, but faster and faster as the searcher lost patience in a quest to find the secret.

"Hah!" A partially-stifled giggle followed with the realization that the hiding place had been located.

The light grew bigger as the figure approached a spot in the wall where the flashlight illuminated a small seam in the paneling. It resembled all the other seams except for a tiny notch that had been surreptitiously carved in the upper-right hand corner of the panel. Anyone else might not have taken notice. Or, if he or she had, it might have been blamed on a defect in the wood.

But the searcher knew it was there for a purpose. The searcher knew it had been placed there to make the hiding compartment easier to find.

Slipping a finger behind the notch, the board moved forward several inches effortlessly, giving access to what was hidden in the wall. A hand moved down the insulation until it should have come upon a thick bump.

Nothing.

Feeling more feverishly now, the hand grasped the panel and yanked it free from the wall.

Nothing.

Looking around the garage, flashlight desperately swinging back and forth across the walls lighting up the corners of all the panels, the figure felt the beginnings of panic creeping toward the outermost edges of awareness.

Where is it? It was here! I put it here so long ago…and now it's gone?

Did someone find it?

If it was found and taken, why didn't they come for me?

Where is it!!!

Alarm turned to something more urgent—fear. The mind started to process the meaning, and fear turned to dread when the realization hit that the secret was no longer hidden, and that someone else knew what happened to Libby Newman.

And who could that someone else be?

"So the blood is human." Marvin said, "What does it mean? Do we have a crime on our hands? Or is it some kid's idea of a prank?"

"Not so fast, Chief," Jim replied, wincing from the pain that even a slight amount of talking caused in his chest. He had let Claire handle most of the summary of the events as they had unfolded the last few days.

Claire put her hand on Jim's arm and took up from where he left off, "We are not assuming anything—yet."

Chief Hennessey started to interrupt.

"Let me finish, Marvin. Maybe someone was injured. Maybe they were doing some illegal hunting in the Conservancy and didn't want anyone to know so they dropped the knife and ran."

"Yeah, but you saw blood first, and then the knife didn't appear until the next day! That doesn't make any sense," Chief replied.

"Why only one set of shoe prints?"

He decided, "Sounds like a stupid prank to me"

"True…and the rose…" She seemed ready to say something else, but decided not to.

"Come on, Claire, I know you better than that," Marvin chided her, "Out with it! What are you thinking?"

"Well," she looked at him and then, Jim.

Jim nodded his head as if to give her reassurance.

"I'm not sure the person who is leaving these clues is…," pausing.

"Claire, for the love of God, what is it!" Chief Hennessey interjected.

"I think Libby Newman is trying to send me a message about her killer! Okay, there you have it! Are you happy?"

Jim cracked a smile but tried hard not to laugh when he saw Marvin's face.

Chief looked at her for the longest time and eventually spoke up, "Her killer! You don't even know if she's dead."

He lowered his head and continued, "You're talking about a dead person! Are you crazy, woman? Has retirement cost you your mind?"

"See, Jim, I told you. He doesn't believe me. Oh no, he doesn't believe one of his best investigators. He thinks I'm a crazy old woman."

Annoyed, Claire folded her arms and sat down hard on the chair next to the window.

"Now that's not fair!" He paused, "Besides, I didn't call you 'old'," Captain Hennessey replied with a grin.

She didn't reply, but only stared at him with disdain.

He attempted to apologize by adding, "I'm sorry, Claire. I didn't mean to dismiss your suspicions but you'll have to admit they're pretty far-fetched for a seasoned state trooper like me to believe."

"Oh, and I'm not!" Claire huffed and folded her arms even tighter, adding, "I didn't even tell you two what happened today."

"What happened?" Jim asked, eyeing her uncertainly.

Reluctantly she responded, "Well...Myra and Kay, my neighbors, were out for a walk and they noticed water bubbling up in my yard, right in the same place where the blood and other things were found."

"Water?"

"Yes, Jim, water...and it was warm...not cold. They thought it might be a water leak, but I don't think so. It's just too strange that warm water would be springing up in the yard, in the same place," she added.

"What do you think it means, Claire?" Chief asked her.

"I don't know, Marvin! That's what I'm trying to decide. I just don't know!"

Jim put his hand in the air and said weakly, "Can I suggest a truce for tonight."

He grimaced and painfully continued, "Could you ask the nurse for some pain pills for me on your way out?"

He put his hand down and added, "But, I'd like to give you some advice, Marvin...listen to her. She makes sense."

Claire motioned with a jerk of her head that Chief should go out and find the nurse.

When he left, she bent down and placed a kiss on Jim's cheek.

Whispering, "Thank you. Get some rest and I'll see you tomorrow."

Jim took her hand and said, "Just be careful. I believe you, but I think you have more than the supernatural to be afraid of."

Claire nodded and backed out of the room. She blew him a kiss, turned around, and ran straight into Marvin Hennessey.

Grinning, he said, "You like him, don't you?"

Claire grabbed his arm and said, "Come on. Let's get out of here before I put you in a hospital bed too!"

"Oooh, that sounds sexy."

"I didn't mean it that way," she punched him in the arm as they walked down the corridor to the parking garage.

CHAPTER FIFTEEN

Grabbing a beer out of the refrigerator, the person took a swig and felt the beginnings of relaxation. He looked around the small but comfortable confines of the apartment and thought about the house. *Sure beats the hell out of this place.*

He frowned when he remembered the judge declaring it her property in the divorce decree. *I wanted to keep the house! It held memories for me too.*

He gulped the last of the beer and threw the can in the wastebasket. *I didn't get all my belongings out either,* he remembered. *That always bothered me, but especially now when I think about everything I left there.*

Startled, he recalled something else. *Wonder if Claire Dungarven knows about my stuff? I wouldn't mind contacting her, but it's been a long time.*

He smiled as he reminisced about that part of his past. *I read something about her in the newspaper recently. She's retired! That's right. She retired from the state police and moved to Brown County. Article said she bought a home at Sweetwater Lakes.*

The man thought about this piece of information, *Wonder if I should pay her a visit and see if she can help me?*

His smile turned sinister. *And, maybe I should find out what she knows.*

After saying goodnight to Marvin and, as she stated, 'agreeing to patronize him in allowing him to check her house before he left', Claire turned on the front porch light and headed for her bedroom.

She glanced in the tiny office and thought fleetingly about writing, but decided she needed the sleep more.

I'll put off until tomorrow what I could do tonight.

She went into the hall bathroom and looked at her reflection in the mirror while grabbing for her toothbrush.

I look tired but my mind is racing a mile a minute!

As she brushed her teeth, she thought about what Jim had told her...*human blood. Whose blood could it be?*

And, more to the point, why is it in my yard?

She considered the possibilities.

Is it just a coincidence or did someone actually have an accident and then walk through my yard dripping blood?

No, that doesn't account for the one set of shoe prints...and the blood showing up before the knife appeared...and the rose.

She finished brushing and wiped her mouth on the towel.

As she washed her face, another thought came to mind.

It has to be deliberate! It's too much like someone is staging a whole collection of clues to build up a scenario for me.

She asked herself, *So, if that's true, what is the person trying to tell me?*

And who is this person who is trying to tell me something?

Then, the recollection of how many similarities there were between the signs found in the yard and the clues in the disappearance of Libby Newman hit her full force again.

The revelation stunned Claire.

It has to be connected to her case! There's no other possible answer.

She remembered, *and then, she came to me in the dream.*

If she's alive, did she attempt to communicate with me telepathically?

"If so, that would be very...bizarre," she answered her own question.

Claire gazed in the mirror for a long time and then her eyes took on a very determined set with the abrupt realization... *She is dead...and she's trying to lead me to her killer!*

As she walked to her bedroom, Claire spoke aloud, "Okay, Libby. Tell me what you need me to know. I'm ready to help."

❖

Later, startled awake in the middle of the night, Claire sat up and tried to remember all that she could about her just-completed dream. Libby had come to her; she signed 'help', but also used pictures to relay a sequence of events.

It's like she's reenacting what happened. Libby saw the door alarm light up; she went to the door and opened it; she frowned slightly; it changed momentarily to a timid smile.

She knew the person!

A hand motioned to come out on the front porch...

"Wait a minute," Claire said, "I'd better get a notebook and write this down. I'll never remember all the details if I don't."

She went into the kitchen and grabbed a tablet off the countertop and reached for a pen in the small jar she kept next to the phone. She sat down at the table and began to write furiously. *Flashing light of the door alarm, hand motioning to come outside...*

After writing everything down, Claire sat back and looked at what she had written.

Knowing that she was not going to sleep the rest of the night, she stood up and grabbed the coffee container out of the cabinet, with intentions to make some strong coffee that would help her be as sharp as she would need to be.

Glancing at the clock, she groaned when she realized how early it was, "4:30 in the morning! It's going to be a long day."

A car crept slowly by the house. The person behind the wheel strained in the darkness to take in the house numbers.

Too dark to see anything...

Agitated at seeing a light flick on in the house, *she's awake!*

Don't want her to notice my lights. I'd better go by, turn around down the street, and hope she doesn't look out the window.

But, if she does, maybe she'll think it's the newspaper carrier.

At least I know where she lives now, the observer added chillingly.

The individual grasped the wheel tighter. *I can keep an eye on her…and, maybe she'll lead me to what I want!*

Tossing, turning, Marvin Hennessey finally gave up the ghost and got out of bed, carefully, quietly, hoping not to disturb Mary. He couldn't get his mind off the information that Claire and Jim had shared with him at the hospital.

It's not that I don't believe her, but I'm trying hard not to ignore the facts…there was blood, one set of shoeprints, and a knife in Claire's front yard…I don't know what that rose and the pool of water mean, but for now I'll try to concentrate on the other evidence…

Walking into the living room, he glanced out the window, attempting to 'set the scene' in his own mind: *Blood, shoeprints and more blood, a knife…and a rose.*

He kept coming back to the flower. It was what didn't make sense. *Why would someone leave a rose? And, it's still fresh, according to Claire. It is strange that a rose would show up in her front yard in the dead of winter. And, what does it mean?*

Marvin sat down in his easy chair and pondered the whole scenario.

Maybe she's right. It sounds like someone is leaving clues to a crime. Like Claire said, Libby did have a rose tattoo on her ankle.

He thought back to all the teasing he gave her and felt a stab of guilt. *I didn't mean to give Claire the impression I don't believe her, but it flies in the face of the common wisdom a police officer usually employs to solve a mystery.*

Then, he sat up straight and thought about the other possibility. *What if it is something supernatural?*

What if Libby Newman is the one leaving the signs in the snow?

If so, where is she and what happened?

"Maybe I need to read the details of that case again," he whispered to himself.

That's what I'll do. I need to go to the office today anyway...clean out my desk, pick up some possessions. I'll just pull it up on the computer and read it again. Maybe something will pop up. Sure can't hurt, Marvin thought as he made his way back to bed.

Chapter Sixteen

At the first sign of dawn's light, Claire stood at the sliding doors, leading to the deck in the back of her house, admiring the sunrise.

What beautiful colors!

Sunrise and sunset had always been two of her favorite times of the day. Until recently she had always had plenty of opportunities to enjoy both since she often worked from early in the morning until late at night. Even on bad days, she tried to stop and enjoy the two stunning natural events even if she was in the middle of a particularly tragic investigation. Now, with retirement, she could enjoy both without having to make time for them. They were just there for her pleasure.

Sipping her coffee, Claire organized her thoughts and made plans for the day ahead.

First, I'll call Jim and see how he's feeling, and if the doctor has released him, I'll see if he wants me to come and bring him home.

Then, if he's up to it, I'll share what I've pieced together from my dream and see if he can help me find this place where Libby might be.

But first, I want to check and see if there are any more clues out front.

Claire turned and walked toward the living room window.

Pushing the curtain aside, she looked out in the yard and thought she saw something else in the snow in the exact same spot where all the other clues had been.

I knew it! I think she's left me another sign, but I need to get a closer look.

She walked to the front door, opened it, and a blast of cold air hit her immediately.

Shivering, she thought, *it's a lot colder today. That new snow last night really brought the temperature down. I'd better get dressed and put on my coat before I go outside.*

She went down the hallway, but paused at the door of the office.

I can get a better view from here, she thought as she went into the room.

She approached and peered out the window, clearly seeing red in the snow. Her hand flew up to her mouth in an attempt to stifle the gasp forming in the back of her throat.

Hurriedly, she left the room and proceeded to the bedroom. Her first order of business was to get dressed and be outside before anything happened to the fresh blood.

Excited, Claire announced over the phone, "I got another sample, Jim. There was more blood out there this morning. I scooped it up and saved it."

Jim listened carefully and asked her, "Did you place it in a container and put it in the freezer before the snow melted?"

"Of course! You're talking to another law enforcement officer, you know," she chided him.

He chuckled and said, "I should have known you would give me grief over that question. Besides, I was just teasing you."

"Yeah, I bet you were!"

He asked her if she could come and pick him up before he went stir crazy and she readily agreed to do it.

Before she hung up though, she informed him that she had more to tell him.

Libby made an appearance in her dream last night and she had made notes of everything she remembered.

She said she had some ideas of what to do next, Jim remembered.

I wonder what those plans include.

Claire had also hinted that she needed his assistance. He certainly hoped that he could help her. She was fast becoming a very important part of his life.

After all these years...

Jim slowly but cautiously got out of bed and began to get dressed.

I just hope I can help her find Libby...and finally give them both some peace.

Someone watching saw Claire drive away.

She didn't even see me. But if she had, she wouldn't have known.

Grinning while recalling the past, the thoughts continued, *it was a lucky break that the other policeman interviewed me. She might have remembered if she had been the one to come. I never had to worry before, but she had the skills. She probably would have figured it out...even with the disguise.*

Considering what had to be done, the watcher decided, *if she gets too close, I'll have to take care of it. She's too clever and I can't risk her finding out the truth.*

A new idea popped into mind though, *think I'll look around while she's gone. Maybe I'll find something.*

If so, maybe I can just disappear again. No one would know and I could move on. No loose ties. Just like before...I could fade away.

It was the middle of the morning before Chief Hennessey could finally sit down at his computer and read the summaries from the Libby Newman case.

Many well-wishers who were unable to attend the retirement party had drifted in and out of his office for the past two hours.

Some just wanted to say good-bye, but some wanted to sit and reminisce about old 'war' stories.

It felt good to share, but he kept watching the clock and wondering if he would find anything of interest when he went through the information that was stored in the computer.

But now the steady stream of visitors had slowed considerably and he was reading through the investigators' files and looking at the pictures.

Hmmm...her ex-husband was a trucker. The picture we have isn't very good but he looks like he would blend in pretty well in any kind of gathering.

In fact, I wish we had a better picture, because with this one, he's wearing a cap and I can't really make out any distinguishing features.

Chief scrolled up through the pictures from the home and couldn't find anything that looked significant.

Nothing out of place.

Strange that she would leave her purse. Women always take their purses with them anywhere they go! That might lead me to think she went hurriedly...not like she was planning this ahead of time.

Marvin read through the interviews from the family, friends and co-workers. *No one felt as if Libby was unhappy...just a little quiet. But, according to all of them, she was a quiet person anyway.*

Seemed a little more withdrawn than usual after the divorce, but that's to be expected.

A couple of them made a comment about being surprised when she married Trent. They just seemed to feel that he was not what they anticipated when Libby showed them his picture.

He was older, but that happens.

He was a hearing man. Maybe they thought she would marry someone who was deaf.

Marvin scrolled back to the picture of Trent. He squinted and focused on the image. *I guess women would say he was handsome...hard to tell.*

What strikes me is that his description is so typical—almost six feet tall, brown hair, brown eyes.

Chief Hennessey sat up straight and looked at the wall across from his desk, trying to remember something that was nagging at him.

He blinked, glanced back at the computer screen, and thought, *maybe that is what's bothering me. He is so...normal, so... 'Everyman' in his looks.*

Suddenly, Marvin's expression changed as the realization hit him that that was exactly why he was pestered by the nondescript object of his scrutiny.

And, he began the process of digging into Trent Newman's past on a much deeper level than the investigators had ever done.

Gently, Claire took Jim by the hand and helped him out of her car. He gave her his house key so she could open the door.

"It's nice to have a woman care for me. It's been a long time."

"Oh yeah, well don't get too used to it."

He laughed and said, "I have a feeling, Claire Dungarven, that you are the kind of person who will make sure I don't get used to it!"

They both entered the house, chattering and trying to take their mind off the elements of mystery that had been playing out for the last few days.

Jim collapsed into a chair while Claire busied herself putting away his medicine and other supplies from the hospital.

At the same time that she was going to ask him where he wanted the medicine, in the kitchen or in the bathroom, the phone rang.

Jim started to get up from his chair but Claire noticed that he still wasn't moving too quickly.

"Do you want me to get that?"

He nodded his head and sat back down.

"Hello."

"This is Shirley Trusty. Is Jim available?"

"Oh, hi Shirley, this is Claire Dungarven."

"Hi, Claire. Sorry to hear about Jim's accident."

She continued, "Is he there? I have some information I wanted to give him."

"Sure. Hold on. I'll see if he can come to the phone."

Jim motioned for Claire to go ahead and take the message.

"He just came home from the hospital, Shirley. Could you give me the message and I'll relay it to him if you don't mind."

"No, that's fine. I just forgot to tell him yesterday that the blood is B positive. That's a fairly rare type of human blood and I wanted him to know it."

Startled, Claire recalled from her recent readings on the investigation that Libby's blood type was B positive.

Taken aback by this piece of news, her voice remained calm and she didn't let on to Shirley, "Okay, thanks for letting us know."

She then added, "Is there anything you can tell us about the knife?"

"Glad you reminded me about that one. I found some fingerprints and then I checked the data base to see if I could make a match."

Claire grasped the phone tightly, "Did you find a match?"

"Yes, as a matter of fact I did, but it was somewhat of a surprise."

Shirley hesitated before proceeding, "The fingerprints are connected to a missing person investigation, one I think you might have been involved with."

"Would it be the Libby Newman disappearance?" Claire waited for a reply, not taking a breath.

"Why, yes it would! How did you guess?"

Claire exhaled and said, "I figured that sooner or later he would turn up."

Shirley paused and then quietly responded, "Who were you thinking it would be, Claire?"

"The ex-husband, Trent Newman…I always knew he was involved…"

Shirley interrupted her, "No, you don't understand. It's not Trent Newman's fingerprints on the knife."

Claire looked puzzled.

Jim watched, trying to gauge where the conversation was headed.

"I'm not sure I know what you mean, Shirley. Whose fingerprints did you find on the knife?"

"The fingerprints belonged to Libby Newman."

For the second time in less than twenty-four hours, Claire dropped the phone.

Jim reacted quickly, considering his injuries. He stood up carefully, walked over, and picked up the phone. He could hear Shirley in the background calling Claire's name.

"I'm sorry, Shirley. We'll get back to you later."

Hanging up the phone, he put his arms around Claire and rubbed her neck. "Calm down. I don't know what Shirley told you but I can tell it wasn't good."

She hung on to Jim and put her head on his shoulder, "The blood type was B positive…and that is Libby's blood type."

Jim said, "I know you're upset, Claire, but we already suspected that she must have been the victim of a crime, and this just proves it."

"True, Jim, but it's what else she told me that really bothers me."

"What did she say?"

"The fingerprints on the knife didn't belong to Trent Newman. They were Libby's."

It wasn't that difficult to gain entry into Claire's home. People in the lakes community were suspicious of any strangers, but recently there had been a number of houses sold to "part-timers", neighbors who were only down for the summer or weekend.

Therefore, residents were becoming used to seeing cars parked in driveways that typically had little traffic.

People were beginning to recognize Claire. She had become a fixture in the neighborhood even though she hadn't lived there that long…but not long enough to know who her friends or visitors might be.

By the time anyone would see me or my car, I'll be long gone, the intruder rationalized.

Breaking the window pane in the back door and looking around to see if anyone was close by, the person was satisfied to realize that the trees hid any activity from view. Then, that individual carefully reached through the broken glass and unlocked the door.

Cautiously, *she'll report this break-in as soon as she comes home so I'll need to allow myself time to clean any fingerprints.*

Taking the stairs two at a time, the individual started in the kitchen, checking the cabinets and drawers.

When that chore was completed, the interloper felt budding impatience.

I can't find it! It should be here in the kitchen! But, it's not! It makes sense to put it in here, but maybe she's hiding it in another part of the house.

Beginning to panic, the prowler started rummaging through the other rooms, realizing this wasn't going to be easy, leaving drawers open, dumping items on the bed, flinging papers around the office.

Watching the clock, irrational behavior increased and resolve to be careful diminished.

The trespasser let out a silent scream, thinking, *I can't leave here without it!*

Then, hesitating for a minute, *I need to think. Where would she put it?*

That person looked out the bedroom window and tried to gather thoughts.

Suddenly, a consideration came to mind. *Maybe she hid it in the freezer. People do that because they think no one will look in a freezer.*

But, reasoning, *she's a retired detective! She'd be a little smarter than that!*

I have to look though, the individual decided, walking toward the kitchen. *Can't hurt...*

And, once in the kitchen, the intruder opened the freezer compartment and looked carefully through the food stored there.

What is this? The individual held up a bag with some snow and something red on it.

It's blood!

Turning it around and peering at it from all angles, *it sure is blood!*

Wonder why anyone would keep it in their freezer?

Making a quick decision, the thief grasped the bag and closed the door. *I'll just have to take it with me and figure it out later.*

The perpetrator hurriedly ran downstairs and out the door, carrying the bag. And, in the curiosity over seeing the bag with snow and blood in it, somebody forgot the resolve to be careful and clean up before leaving Claire's house.

CHAPTER SEVENTEEN

"Okay, Claire, let me get this straight." Jim leaned back in his easy chair after listening to Claire's description of her latest dream.

"Libby saw the flashing light on her door that alerted her to somebody knocking. She went to the door and opened it. Then, she went outside to greet this visitor, but you didn't see the person in the dream, right?"

"No, and that is a concern to me because she never did show me who it was. She kept the identity a secret...and I don't know why. If someone took her, why didn't she reveal it to me in the dream?"

Jim hesitated before replying, "Let's not worry about that for now because we're not even sure what happened to her yet. But if she showed you this sequence in a dream, what would be her motivation?"

Claire threw up her hands before placing them on her knees, "I don't know, Jim. That's what doesn't make sense to me!"

"Continue on with the details. Let's see if I can help you," he requested.

Claire cleared her throat and began again, "She left with someone that night. It seemed as if she knew who it was because her expression was one of familiarity. She followed this 'somebody' to a location where there was a power utility substation close to her house.

We already knew that because the footprints led to this location," Claire explained. "The shoeprint impression left in my yard was probably referring to this part."

She added, "But I didn't know what happened next, and Libby gave me more information in the dream."

Jim motioned for Claire to resume.

"She showed me a motorcycle. She got on the back and took off with whoever was driving the bike."

"At the time we thought a male was involved with Libby's disappearance because we have the larger shoeprints and they match a type and brand of shoe that is popular with guys, but other than that, we have nothing else," Claire ended.

Jim asked, "In the dream did she show you where they went?"

"Yes, but most of what I could see was water. She indicated that she was close to a body of water," Claire replied. "That explains the water in my yard…"

He interrupted, "Could you tell, from what you saw, where this place might be?"

"I'm not sure but I might be able to locate it," Claire answered.

She wavered before continuing, "I think I recognized the surroundings. It might be close to Pine Lake."

Jim gave her a questioning stare.

She explained, "There were a lot of pine trees in the background. My Dad used to take me fishing there. He…"

Persevering, Jim said, "Focus on the dream, Claire. Just think about what she showed you."

Deep in thought now, Claire added, "and there was a short but overgrown path, leading to a dock. The dock was pretty rickety. There was an old canoe, tipped up on its side, next to the dock. Grass was growing up around it, like it had been there for a while. She…she looked at the water, but then she extended her arm and pointed to the trees."

By way of explanation, Claire said, "All in all there are some pretty remote areas around that lake…"

"I'm familiar with Pine Lake," Jim said. "I think we could find it, with those details, and both of us looking.

He asked, "Would you want to go and scout around?"

Claire paused and then replied, "I want to check it out, Jim, but first I have some other questions that are bothering me…and they need to be answered before we can move forward."

"What questions, Claire?"

"Well, for starters, I want to know why she came to me in a dream. Why would she do that if she's still alive?"

Jim shook his head, "That's something I can't answer either."

Claire continued in a rush, "Because if she's alive, why wouldn't she just write, call, or come and see me? If she's being held against her will, how could she still be alive after all this time? What is the significance of this place near water? Why the blood? And, finally, how can someone who is dead leave fingerprints on a knife?"

At this barrage of questions, Jim threw his hands up, as stumped by the incongruity of the findings as Claire was.

She looked at him, "Where is she? What happened to her? She's left out all the answers to the most burning questions."

He stared back at her before lowering his head, "I don't know, Claire, but I think I know someone who might be able to help if you want to go and see her."

"If someone has information that can help us find Libby, I'm all for it!"

Puzzled, she continued, "Why didn't you say something before?

He sat there with his head down, hands clasped together, not answering.

Restlessly, she asked him another question, "Who is this person you're talking about?"

Jim grimaced but said, "You might laugh at me when you hear what I'm about to say, but give it a chance."

"What do you mean by that?" Claire looked at him quizzically.

"Her name is Lynn Brookmeier. Have you ever heard of her?"

"No, should I?"

"Maybe," he paused, "but I don't know if you'll want to talk to her."

"For God's sake, Jim," she replied rather quickly. "Why wouldn't I want to talk to her if she has information about Libby?"

"Well, there's one thing you need to know…," he wavered as if he was considering how best to answer her.

Claire gestured her hands toward him in an impatient manner and said, "Out with it! What?"

"She's a… psychic."

❖

Captain Marvin Hennessey hung up the phone and stared at his desk.

I can't imagine a trucking company that would hire someone, have that person work for them for years, and not know any background. That's just crazy!

He sighed, *but unfortunately it happens all the time. And now, it's making information more difficult to come by.*

He smiled when he remembered what he had told Claire recently. *She'll tease me unmercifully when she finds out how hard I'm working on this...and I just retired!*

Shaking his head, *state police are a bunch of workaholics and they don't know how to retire!*

He put on his glasses and prepared to do more research on the computer.

Funny thing...This Trent Newman seems to have no past. According to the personnel director at Landry trucking company, Mr. Newman just showed up one day and they gave him a job. At least that's what it sounded like.

Chief Hennessey remembered the request he made over the phone.

About that time the fax number rang and he hoped that it was the information he had asked for.

If there's anything helpful in his records, it will show up in the application he submitted when he first began working there...or at least give me a starting point, because right now I've hit a roadblock.

Marvin thought back to the information he had read in the police reports so far. *Evidently this Newman character didn't make a good impression on Libby's family or friends. At least he didn't share much information about himself. According to them, he did say he was adopted and his adoptive parents were dead; no brothers or sisters; no previous marriages that we know about.*

He collected the papers from the fax machine and started to read. *Has worked at Landry Trucking for seven years; good record there so far, according to the contact...*

Suddenly he shot up in his chair as he read over the list of references that Trent Newman had written on his resume.

Claire Dungarven! Why would he have Claire listed as a reference?

This is getting very strange! I think I'd better call that personnel director back and ask him if they ever checked his references. How would Trent Newman know Claire?

As the intruder sped away from Claire's house, a fog-like substance began to grow and take shape. It evolved slowly into an ethereal being, watching and waiting in the woods, wishing for her to come back home.

Not much time left.

The ghostly figure seemed to bend in response to the wind in the trees.

I need to tell the whole story.

Hidden, the spirit blended in with the snowy backdrop so well that anyone who happened to look out their window or drive by in a car would think that the wind had picked up the snow and made it dance in the icy afternoon sunlight.

It has to be soon or they won't find me. Someone is making sure of that!

The wisp seemed to respond more fervently as agitation grew.

What am I going to do now? The clue is gone!

The white form fluttered, acknowledging the chilly breeze, or maybe was it fear? Growing dread? Or, a feeling of hopelessness?

I must lead them to my place.

"A psychic!" Claire exclaimed. "You think a psychic can help me with this case?" Exasperatedly she ran her fingers through her hair while staring down Jim.

"Now Claire, it's just a suggestion," he responded.

She plunged ahead, oblivious to his attempt to explain, "I can't believe you would want me to see a psychic!"

She continued, a little calmer, "It's just that I didn't expect that from you…but I can see what you're telling me."

Claire considered the idea and the possibility of discovering new information about the case.

"You know what, you might have something there," she reluctantly agreed.

She walked in circles around the living room, "If she is dead, Libby might come through, with the help of this psychic, and tell us more. And, if she's still alive, maybe Lynn can help us find her."

"That's what I've been trying to tell you, Claire," Jim replied.

She looked at him and asked, "Have you used her before…on a case I mean."

Jim grinned as he answered her question, "Yes, I've used her before on a case and she proved to be very helpful."

"Well, are you going to tell me about it?" She put her hands on her hips and planted herself in front of the chair Jim was sitting in.

He took a deep breath before answering, "About eight years ago we had a suspicious fire here in the Conservancy. Do you remember hearing about that, Claire?"

She nodded affirmatively and motioned for him to continue.

"We found a body in the ruins. It was burned badly—beyond recognition." Jim stopped talking and grimaced at the tragic details and horrible images of the story that the recollections brought up.

He shook his head glumly and resumed speaking, "We presumed it was the owner, but after checking through his background, we found bad credit; he was about to lose his house; his finances were a disaster. By that time, his wife had cremated what was left of the remains and buried the urn in the family plot.

Therefore, DNA wasn't available and besides, testing wasn't as sophisticated as it is now."

"That happens, but what made you think it wasn't him?"

"We heard rumors of sightings, after the fire, around the county. But you know how people can be. They think they see someone and then it pans out not to be true."

"But, people who knew him were hinting that he might have planned what looked like his own death. He probably thought he could collect on the life insurance, with the help of the wife, who was home at the time of the fire and ran to the neighbors for help."

Jim added, "She was acting very suspiciously too."

"How so?"

"Well, she rented a small place in a rural area, but stayed in the county after the fire. When we would go out to talk with her, she never let us in the house. She'd always see us coming and walk out on the porch to speak with us," Jim explained.

"Of course, a lot of people who live here have a distrusting attitude toward the police, but she seemed extra cautious."

"Did you ever see him yourself?"

"No, but we couldn't ignore the rumors that were running rampant, so we decided to take a more drastic approach."

"And you called on this Lynn Brookmeier," Claire added.

"Exactly, and we were surprised at the answers she gave us."

"What did she tell you?"

Jim leaned forward in the chair, "She told us that he was not dead."

Claire raised her eyebrows at this revelation, "Was she able to tell you where he might be?"

"Unfortunately, she wasn't getting enough clear information to tell us his location."

He stopped, as if remembering something, and then proceeded, "Lynn said she was seeing him, but the picture was murky and confusing; she couldn't get a distinct image of where he was." Jim felt a nagging sensation pricking at his consciousness, just out of reach.

"I remember reading in the newspaper about the search to find him, but can't recall hearing anything about that piece of the puzzle. Didn't the wife file to have him declared legally dead last year?"

The uneasy feeling Jim had began to fade as he concentrated on the question and replied, "Yes, and we had to give up our search. Haven't had reports of any sightings since those initial ones. He just evaporated into thin air; she's gone too; she moved to Tennessee and we haven't heard anything from her since she had him declared legally dead, just vanished...no one knows where she is now. Maybe they're together again, but we'd probably have to showcase it on "America's Most Wanted" to get any new leads on their whereabouts," Jim surmised.

"Sounds frustrating," Claire replied.

"Extremely, because we've lost track of both of them."

"Very cunning," she said, "but one of these days you'll find them. He can't hide forever."

"That's what we're hoping," Jim agreed.

Claire sat down on the couch, thought about what Jim had told her, and decided, "Okay, I'll go see Lynn. Maybe she can at least tell me if Libby is dead or alive. It's worth a shot," she reasoned.

Jim pointed to the kitchen, "I have her phone number in my address book. It's in the kitchen next to the phone. Could you bring it to me?"

Claire stood up and walked over to the kitchen while responding, "Sure, but I really want you to go with me. Do you feel well enough to do it if she says to come over today?"

He nodded and said, "I think we'd better, as soon as possible." His expression was disquieting.

"Are you sure? You don't look good, Jim."

"Yes," he told her, "In fact, I have a real sense of urgency."

He frowned as he tried to focus on the bothersome impressions that were filling his mind again, and hesitated before telling her the next part, "Libby wants us to know the truth."

CHAPTER EIGHTEEN

"So, you didn't check any of the references provided on the application form?"

"Yes, Captain Hennessey, that's right," the voice on the other end of the phone responded. "We needed someone right away and he had the experience so we hired him."

"Haven't been disappointed either. He's been a good employee," the personnel director, Mr. Cane, added somewhat defensively.

Marvin rubbed his forehead, trying to prevent the headache that was forming from becoming any worse. "So, you wouldn't know if he mentioned this Claire Dungarven to you personally. Or, do you ever overhear him talking about her?"

"Nope, can't say I do. Of course, he isn't in the office much. I don't get many opportunities to talk to him. Plus," he added, "He's not much of a talker, pretty much a loner, doesn't have many friends that I know of."

"Any family?"

"No...," Mr. Cane paused as if considering whether to bring something up or not, then he continued, "He used to bring up his wives, but now that they are both gone, he doesn't talk about family."

Marvin grasped the phone tighter; a breath caught in his throat. "What do you mean his wives?" The knuckles on his right hand grew whiter as he increased his hold on the receiver. "His wife, Libby Newman, disappeared four years ago but she was his only wife."

Surprised, Mr. Cane responded, "Didn't you know he was married before? I always thought it was strange that a man could lose two wives in the same way."

Chief felt his heart skip a beat as he asked, "He lost two wives in the same way?"

"They both disappeared; he told me. Up and left him. I kinda' felt sorry for him; some of the other guys did too when I told them, but he didn't mention it again. It was like he regretted telling me. Guess he felt embarrassed that two women would leave him like that."

Marvin interrupted him, "Mr. Cane, I think we need to talk in person. Could I come and see you?"

"You mean <u>now</u>?"

"Yes, the sooner the better," Chief Hennessey replied, hanging up the phone.

A blast of cold air hit Claire and Jim as they exited the back door of his house. Briskly, they walked to the car, partly due to the cold, but also because of their growing excitement at the prospect of visiting Lynn Brookmeier.

When Claire opened the car door for Jim, she noticed the anguished look on his face and tenderly asked, "Are you sure you want to do this today? We could wait until tomorrow. I can call her back."

Jim shook his head adamantly, "No, we need to see her today." He grimaced before continuing, "I'm not clear why, but I get the feeling that we need to hurry."

He held onto a bottle of water as he climbed into Claire's car. Clasping the seatbelt on, he fished a pain pill out of his jacket pocket and gulped it down with a drink of the liquid.

Worriedly, Claire glanced over at him as she sat behind the wheel and put on her seatbelt. "Are you hurting?"

Jim pushed aside her concern but answered, "I'm only taking one of these because I want to be sharp when we hear what she has to say."

He motioned for her to start the car.

Claire turned the key and put the car in reverse, all the while sneaking anxious peeks at Jim. "Lynn said to bring something of Libby's for her to inspect, right?"

Jim nodded his head, pain evident on his face.

"Since we're in a hurry, I'll stop by and get the blood out of the freezer," Claire said. "We know it's her blood type; chances are it's hers; and maybe Lynn can pick up on something using that."

"Otherwise," she continued, "we would have to drive to Frederick again."

Jim waved his hand dismissively, "Not enough time for that. Just use the blood. Something tells me it's hers too."

Claire looked at him strangely and started to say something, but decided to let it drop.

"I'm sorry, Claire," Jim finally said, "It's just that I keep getting this persistent feeling that we don't have much time left."

"Time for what? Time to get the case solved?"

Faltering, "I think Libby is sending us a message."

"What kind of message?"

Jim replied, "I think she's trying to tell us that we need to find her and solve this case before someone else disappears...or is murdered."

The bag of snow, covered with blood stains, sat on the passenger car seat; the driver stole numerous glances at it.

Whose blood is it?

The individual, who was also the sole occupant of the car, strived to keep attention on the road while uneasily pondering this question.

She's a retired police officer. Maybe it was in the freezer as evidence in a crime.

Uncertainty set in at this suggestion and creased lines appeared around the mouth and on the forehead.

But why would she have evidence in her own freezer? Usually they store it at a crime lab.

Eyebrows shot up. *And, not to forget, she's retired now. Why put blood in your freezer if not for a case you're working on currently?*

"It just doesn't make sense!" The sentiment spoken aloud contributed to the car's occupant temporarily losing concentration. A horn brought back full attention as instinct caused the driver to turn the wheel sharply to the right, narrowly missing another car coming in the opposite direction.

Taking a stab at wry humor, *I'm reacquainting myself with the 'local' bad habits, crossing the center line, oblivious to oncoming traffic.*

Frowning, but remembering to be cautious, *it wouldn't do me any good to be stopped by the Conservancy police...especially with this bag and its contents sitting in my front seat!*

The person in the car then had another thought, *why hang onto it? What good does it do me to keep it?*

In fact, a sudden realization hit, *why did I take it? I need to get rid of it! I don't want even a hint of suspicion to lead them to me!*

Proceeding out of the lakes area, the individual in the car looked in the rearview mirror, saw no other cars following, looked on either side, only saw woods, and made a hasty decision.

Slowing down, the driver pushed the power button to open the window. A hand grabbed the bag of red blood-stained snow and heaved it out, watching until it landed amongst the trees.

Finally a smile appeared, worry gave way to relief, and the car picked up momentum, as a foot aggressively pushed on the accelerator, bringing the speed back to normal, and once again eyes focused on the road ahead.

Stationed in the woods, a filmy white almost transparent being observed the car as it drove away. Looking sadly down at the discarded bag that had landed nearby, an anguished expression gave way to determination.

It's imperative I tell them now! I can't let my killer get away! Claire and Jim are the only ones who can help me. I just hope that they believe in ghosts.

As Trent drove up to the front entrance of Landry Trucking, he noticed a state police cruiser parked in front of the office. He looked at the car suspiciously and thought, *wonder why they're here? Surely they can't be bothering them with more questions.*

He frowned uncertainly, grappling with the meaning of the visit. *Maybe they're here because of an accident. Yeah, that must be it. There's always an officer coming out to trucking companies to follow up on accident investigations.*

Trent smiled in an attempt to relax, *don't need to get all shook up about them being here. I know they have plenty of new cases to work on.*

He continued, *they sure ask plenty of questions about accidents though.*

Remembering an incident from a few years ago, *why, I didn't think they'd ever make up their minds about that one!*

Of course, he added, *they're always extra cautious when investigating accidents where one of their own is involved.*

Lucky for me, they didn't find any evidence to link my truck to it!

And besides, Trent heaved a sigh of relief, *that was three years ago.*

He shook his head, *they never did find out what really happened.*

He turned toward the parking lot and walked over to his truck, giving a backward glance toward the office just as the two men exited the office. A worried expression crept onto his face. *When I go in to get my paperwork, I'll ask Art Cane what this is all about. He'll tell me.*

"Thanks for coming with me, George," Marvin said. "This way it looks more official since I'm supposed to be retired."

George Stanley slapped his former co-worker on the back and replied, "No problem, Chief. When you told me that this guy had Claire down as a reference, I couldn't believe it! I had to hear for myself and...," he stopped talking. "Isn't that Trent Newman over there?"

Marvin Hennessey looked in the direction where George was pointing and responded, "Yep, that's him. Looks like he's getting ready to leave on another trip."

"Do you want to talk to him now?"

Chief hesitated before answering, "No, let's get to Claire first. I want to see if she can shine any light on this mystery before we talk to him. And," he added, "I don't want to give him any reasons to think we suspect him of anything at this point."

George nodded in agreement, "You've got the picture. She might recognize him from that, but she didn't do the interviewing of the husband so she might not remember what he looks like."

He continued, "After Brad questioned him, we all had some nagging doubts but couldn't find any evidence linking him to the crime. So, we left it at that and eventually filed it under cold cases. Claire might have gone back to the files and revisited it, but I'm not sure. If she did, and she knew this guy, undoubtedly she would have said something."

Marvin interrupted, "She might have been struck by his description same as I was and not paid much attention to the picture. After all, it's not very clear...he has a cap on and you can't make out his features very clearly."

"What are you talking about, Chief? What struck you about his description? Why wouldn't she have paid attention to the picture?"

He thought about his impressions before explaining, "This guy seems so much like anyone else of that age and background...weight, height, both average, no identifying marks like tattoos or scars, nothing out of the ordinary. When reading the file today, I even gave him a name that typifies someone with features like his."

George gave him a questioning look, "What name?"

"Everyman. His looks do not stand out and that is why he worries me."

"What does that mean?"

Marvin paused before answering, "I mean that Trent Newman could very well be a more complicated individual than we had previously thought."

"In what ways?"

"In lots of ways, George, but specifically I'm concerned that Trent Newman might have the capability to be more than one person...and that's why I want to delve into his past a little more before I send up any red flags that he might detect."

"So, you think he might have been involved with Libby Newman's disappearance?"

Marvin shook his head affirmatively.

"And you think he might have committed other crimes that we need to investigate, like what happened to this supposed first wife?"

Again, Chief Hennessey agreed.

"And," George continued, "You think he might have had the capability to disguise his identity?"

"All of us have that capability, George, but an 'everyman' can pull it off better than anyone else."

Both men stood outside the trucking company office, pondering this possibility until the noonday sun burned their faces a beet-red color.

The ramifications of their thoughts hung like the heavy dust particles kicked up by the traffic in and around the parking lot, suspended in the heat, only moving when a quick sharp breeze left them fluttering. But when the wind died down, the particles would still be there...and so would the implications of what an 'everyman' can do.

CHAPTER NINETEEN

"Oh, my God," Claire gasped as she noticed the broken window in the back door. She turned to see if Jim was watching. He had his head down and seemed to be oblivious to her activities.

She quickly ran up the stairs and looked around her living room, kitchen and dining room.

In complete disarray, her house showed the typical signs of a break-in. Mail and other paperwork to be completed ordinarily lay on the dining room table waiting for attention. Now they were strewn about the floor like the aftermath confetti from a parade.

Kitchen drawers were open and some utensils and silverware were heaped in scattered piles on countertops.

From her vantage point in the middle of the great room combination, she noticed that the drawers in the two living room end tables had been left open and dangled precariously close to dropping on the carpet.

Her organized streak almost took over as she thought about placing the drawers back into their slots, but then, her detective skills assumed responsibility as she reasoned that she didn't need to disturb any of the 'crime scene'.

Quickly moving down the hall, she looked in all three bedrooms and noted that they too had been violated.

At least those are the words she chose to use for the unwanted intrusion into her personal belongings. *Now I know what it feels like to be robbed,* she mused.

Quietly, but alarmingly, another troubling thought entered her mind, *the blood! I wonder if it's still there.* She reversed her pattern of movement and headed back towards the kitchen.

Opening the freezer door, she was met with confirmation of her anxiety—the bag with the blood and snow in it was gone!

Now what am I going to do?

She sat down at the kitchen table and put her hands under her chin, trying to settle her mind and concentrate on a plan.

I need to report it but I also want to see this psychic and find out what she can tell us.

She put her head down on the table when she realized, *I have nothing to show her now! What can we do?*

Her head shot up at the thought, and the realization that followed, *Jim's waiting in the car and is probably wondering what is taking me so long!*

She steadied herself, and after a few seconds, decided to see the psychic first before telling Jim about the break-in.

If he asks, I'll have to tell him. Then, when we arrive at Lynn's house, if she asks, I'll just explain what happened and trust that she can help us.

I hope she's as good as Jim says she is, because with no item to show, we'll be challenging her abilities to their limits!

Claire rushed down the stairs and out to the waiting car, still formulating how she would tell Jim about this latest mishap.

Claire jumped in the car and put it in reverse, her concentration on driving. All the while Jim eyed her warily, waiting for a response.

"Uh, Claire, I noticed you didn't bring anything with you when you came out of your house." He paused, watching her face for an answer. When she remained quiet, he asked, "You did get it, right?"

She looked over at him guiltily and mouthed the word 'no'.

He sat up straighter and winced in response to the sudden movement, "What do you mean 'no'? Why not?" His voice trailed off at the end of the question as another sharp twinge hit his cracked ribs.

Claire glanced over at him with concern written all over her face, "Are you sure you're okay? I can see your injuries are really bothering you. Do you want to go through with this?"

Jim saw right through her attempt to divert the conversation, gritted his teeth more out of frustration and worry than pain, and asked, "What's wrong, Claire? Why didn't you bring the bag?"

Carefully and nervously she studied him before offering an answer, "Well…it…it wasn't there."

He looked at her incredulously, "It wasn't there! What happened to it?"

Sighing, Claire replied, "My house was ransacked, okay. Someone took it."

Jim started to speak but she put up her hand and said, "Look, I know I should have called you to come in and see it but we need to get some answers from Lynn. Let's worry about this later. We need to see if she can help us."

Claire continued, "I'm banking on her being able to pick up on something without having an item belonging to Libby. At least, that's what I'm hoping for," her voice grew quieter with this last pronouncement.

Jim sat in silence for what seemed an eternity before calmly responding, "Okay, but promise me one thing."

"What's that, Jim?"

He reached up and stroked the side of her face, "Promise me that if Lynn gives us a name or description, you'll not go by yourself to find the perp."

Claire reached up and took his hand from her face, kissing it before she laid it down on the seat between them. She looked over at him and said, "Not without you, Jim. Not without you."

She smiled and added, "I have a funny feeling that's a 'given' from now on."

Dust kicked up clouds, obscuring the tiny office and parking lot for a few seconds. When it cleared, a truck was seen speeding away from what was now a vacant lot. No other trucks dotted the landscape, with their engines running, awaiting their drivers to take them to various destinations.

It was early afternoon and few if any drivers would have been stopping in for a run. Most of them would have already been out on the road, delivering their goods, anticipating how long it would take them to complete their assignments and get back home for a few days' rest.

Only the trucker who was the last to leave would have known the truth of what happened at Landry Trucking that afternoon, and if asked, he would claim ignorance about the facts of what happened there, and deny even being present at that time of the day.

Inside the building all was quiet; it looked vacant to the casual observer, but on closer inspection, someone looking through the window would have wondered why no one was inside.

That person might have checked the window to ensure that the "Open" sign was displayed, and once he was reassured that it was still up, he would make his way into the office and take care of whatever business he had.

But if the sign posted read "Closed", like it did now, he would have scratched his head and made his way back to his car, disappointed and maybe a little upset that he was unable to complete his purpose for coming here in the first place.

He might have turned around and headed back to the door to try the lock. Possibly it would have been open; if not, he would surely try calling on his cell phone, on the off chance that someone might have been in there.

And, if that was true, someone might have been able to help him before he left, even though that person could have had a very good reason for placing the "Closed" sign on the window.

Maybe there was a sole occupant and he/she needed to go to the bathroom and didn't want someone entering the building until the nature call was completed.

Perhaps inventory was taking place, but if that was true, an explanation should have been displayed on the sign.

Or, maybe the office was just 'closed'.

But if so, why? It was the middle of the week, the middle of the day, and it should have been business as usual.

101

All of this could have happened…but it didn't.

It was a slow day; the trucks that were assigned were gone; drivers were home or on a trip; no one stopped by for the rest of the day.

But there <u>was</u> somebody in the office, and it would have been hard to see the person if you had just peered in the window.

Why? Was the person hiding? Trying to complete work without interruption?

The answer would not have been crystal clear until later that night, after people were at home, the workday was done, and a wife sat by the phone, looked out the window, and wondered why her husband hadn't called or arrived home with an explanation as to why he was so late.

George and Marvin sat side-by-side, staring intently at the computer screen. Both were reading the information regarding Trent Newman's background. It was in the summary of the interview given to the officer at the time of the investigation.

Sitting on Marvin's lap was the folder with the facts taken from Mr. Newman's resume that Landry Trucking had provided.

Confused, George frowned and made an observation, "It doesn't give us much detail, Marvin."

"Yeah," hesitating before he responded, "it looks like he was being very careful not to give too much information about his past."

"You'd almost think this guy didn't exist until less than ten years ago!"

Chief Hennessey continued to read, "True, everything in here relates to work history; nothing about his personal life, no mention of another wife."

He glanced at George, "Very strange…it appears that Trent Newman had some things he wanted to hide."

"We do have fingerprints. Did we ever run them through the national database?"

Marvin scrolled up through the rest of the investigation summary and read, "No physical evidence from the scene other than the shoe prints. The decision was made not to run the prints through the data base since Mr. Newman was ruled out as a suspect in his wife's disappearance."

"Well that answers the question. I guess they checked out his alibi and were sufficiently assured that he was where he said he was and had nothing to do with his wife's disappearance...or decided that a crime hadn't even been committed."

George Stanley leaned back in his chair, locked his hands behind his neck, and gazed up at the ceiling. "But what if he could be implicated in other crimes?"

He stared thoughtfully at Marvin. "Suppose he does have something to hide? The report says that he was very reluctant to give us any prints or even a picture of himself. When prodded and threatened with a subpoena, he finally provided a photograph and had his fingerprints taken, but he didn't like it."

George continued, "In the summary it says that he asked a lot of questions about why we needed them and how they were to be used."

"I know. That bothered me," Chief Hennessey replied, "but I made the decision to accept what he offered because I really wasn't convinced that any harm had come to his wife. At the time it looked like she had just up and left...decided she wanted a better life somewhere else."

He decided, "I guess I made some conclusions that I shouldn't have. I thought maybe she didn't want to be found."

George replied, "Look, you didn't know, Chief, and any one of us has made decisions that we might regret later, but we do what we have to do at the time."

"True...but that's not helping us now."

He sighed and added, "Let's run those prints through the database and see what we get."

CHAPTER TWENTY

"Thank God, you're here," a frazzled woman opened the door to Claire and Jim standing on her front porch. "Please come in," she continued. "I'm sorry. Sometimes I get a little impatient when I have so much to tell someone."

Claire glanced at Jim and raised her eyebrows.

"You must think I'm just a crazy old woman." She extended her hand to Claire and said, "Lynn Brookmeier, and you must be Claire?"

Shaking hands, "Yes, and I'm pleased to meet you and thank you for allowing us to come today." Claire tried to smile but felt a certain sense of uneasiness.

"Don't worry about me," Lynn answered, "Jim can tell you that I can get flustered, especially if I've received some information from the spirit world and they want me to give it to you as soon as possible."

Claire looked at Jim and said, "Oh…Uh, I guess that means we should get started."

Motioning for them to come into the house, "There's certainly enough time for me to show some politeness instead of any rudeness I'm unintentionally sending your way."

Lynn indicated the couch in the living room for Jim and Claire. She herself took the large, overstuffed recliner facing the two of them.

Both of them perched precariously on the couch, not sliding back into the softness of the cushions, but choosing instead to remain forward in anticipation of what Lynn might tell them.

Lynn sat still with her eyes closed. For several seconds Claire and Jim waited for a comment. When it seemed as if she was not going to speak, she simultaneously sat up, pushed the footstool back in, and stared at both of them before beginning. "I have never had such a sleepless night as I did last night."

She closed her eyes again and breathed in and out as if to steady herself before continuing, "A young woman came to me in my dreams. She…she didn't talk…only gestured. She showed me pictures and tried to make me understand what she was communicating."

Jim interrupted, "What kind of communication was she using?"

Lynn sat quietly, eyes still closed, and finally responded, "I only know the alphabet but it looked like sign language to me."

Claire gasped and put her hand up to her mouth.

Lynn opened her eyes and stared at her for the longest time, "So, she is deaf."

Claire nodded and Lynn continued. "She spelled out her name and it was…let me see if I can do this." She then began to make movements with her fingers…L…i…b…b…y. "I looked it up in a sign language book I have and it spells Libby."

Again Claire gasped.

Jim sat in silence watching the interplay between the two women with growing interest, but indicated with a nod of his head that this was correct.

"She really seemed anxious for me to share this with you," Lynn explained before continuing, "She showed me a place. It was very isolated but I feel like it's not too far from here."

"Can you describe it to us?" Claire leaned even further forward.

"It is outdoors, trees all around, with a body of water." Lynn elaborated, with eyes closed, "There is a small boat…maybe a rowboat or canoe…Wait…Yes, a canoe… next to a dock."

Claire glanced over at Jim but he didn't notice because he was staring intently at Lynn.

"She kept pointing to the trees…"

Claire broke in, "Did she give you a name for this place?"

Lynn thought for a few seconds and shook her head, "No, she didn't give me a name, but the trees might be a clue."

"What do you mean?"

"The trees…they were mostly pine trees."

Claire and Jim looked at each other knowingly before motioning for Lynn to continue.

She sighed heavily and said, "She's dead and she really wanted you to know that."

A small tear glistened in Claire's right eye. "I…I thought as much…but I wasn't sure." She stared at a space in front of her and tried hard to fight off any more tears.

Lynn reached over and grabbed Claire's hand, "She wants you to find her…and something else she wants." Lynn stopped talking.

Claire squeezed her hand, encouraging her to proceed.

"She wants you to find her killer."

Trent Newman held on tightly to the steering wheel of his truck. His thoughts were jangled and fierce. Nightmares had been invading his sleep for too many nights lately. Fighting off sleep he struggled to maintain his composure and concentrate on what he needed to do.

I have to get this delivery made so I'll have my alibi. I'll just tell them when I left Landry this morning, everything was fine. I already had my paperwork, so I didn't even go into the office; no one but me around; no witnesses. Besides, he justified, *what motive would I have?*

He smiled, thinking about it, *so easy.*

But then, his smile faded, *but I need to decide what I'm going to do about Claire. She knows too much…and she's getting too close to the truth.*

Trent nodded his head approvingly as he formulated a plan.

First I make the delivery…and then I'll go see Claire. When I get home, I'll follow her wherever she goes. Maybe she'll lead me to what she knows. And if she does, I'll make sure she doesn't tell anyone else…my sweet Claire. He shook his head sadly and then quickly his expression changed. Frowning, *and if Jim Hoppes is with her, I'll have to take care of both of them.*

Trent glared menacingly at the road ahead, *He knows too much about me already...and he doesn't need to know any more...because if he finds out who I really am, he'll put the whole puzzle together.* Shaking his head, *No, can't allow that to happen. It's been a secret for too long.*

George Stanley and Marvin Hennessey sat across from each other in the break room at the state police office. Sipping coffee, George asked, "So, are you going home soon, or should Mary file a missing person report on you?"

"Cute, George," Chief Hennessey replied. He took another drink of coffee before adding, "I called her earlier and said I would be home in time for supper."

George raised his eyes in response and said, "And she believed that?"

Laughing, "No, she knows me too well."

"She probably wonders why we even gave you a retirement party if you had no intention of retiring."

"Do you want your money back, George?" Marvin smiled at him.

The door to the lounge opened and Trooper Clark Tomlinson spoke to both of them, "Got the results on the fingerprints. We got a match."

Both men pushed away from the table and stood up hurriedly.

"What do you wanna bet he'll be involved in other crimes?" Talking over his shoulder to Marvin, George walked down the hall quickly, eager to see the outcome.

"No bets," Marvin responded quietly, rushing to keep up with the two younger men.

"Do you think it's the same guy?" Officer Tomlinson asked both of his superior officers, turning from one to the other.

George shrugged his shoulders and replied, "Just wait. We'll see soon enough."

George and Clark reached the computer screen before Captain Hennessey and stood there just staring.

Marvin walked up behind them and peered over their shoulders, "What's the conclusion? Is it our guy?"

George moved over so Chief could stand beside them, "I guess you could say it's our guy, Marvin, but there's something else you should see."

Captain Hennessey moved in closer to read the computer screen, staring at it for the longest time before he said anything. "I see what you mean, George. We have a problem…a big problem."

Corporal Stanley stood there with his hands on his hips, not talking, only looking at the screen.

Finally Clark Tomlinson broke their silence, "Okay, would you two let me in on this 'problem'?"

Both men stared at him before Marvin finally responded, "Well, Clark, both George and I saw Trent Newman this morning, and according to the match, we are looking at the fingerprints of a dead man."

Lynn, Claire and Jim sat around the kitchen table, sipping their coffee, waiting for nightfall. Earlier, Lynn had requested that they have a séance and see if Libby would come and give them more information on what to do next. Jim and Claire readily agreed to stay and participate in the séance.

Claire had already asked Lynn about the fingerprints on the knife and how they could belong to someone who was dead. Lynn explained that spirits had been known to leave what were called 'imprints' in the environment. These imprints could possibly include fingerprints, especially if the spirit wanted to leave an impression that she was still around and aware of what was going on in this world.

When asked about the blood on the knife, Lynn surmised that it could also be an example of an imprint. In fact, all of the signs left in the snow could be imprints, especially since they might have been left to symbolize a very traumatic act of violence.

Still digesting these disturbing pieces of information, Claire swirled the remaining coffee around in her cup, gazing down in it as if the pattern it was making would give her clues, like the tea leaves psychics sometimes use.

Lynn watched her and smiled, "Don't bother, Claire. You can't get information from coffee grounds."

Claire looked at her in surprise, "How did you know that's what I was thinking?"

Lynn raised her eyebrows.

Claire abruptly recognized the intent of Lynn's raised eyebrows, and with a wave of her hand, dismissed the question and went back to studying the grounds in the bottom of the cup. Staring hard, she gradually set her cup down on the table and said, "I keep thinking there's something I'm missing on this case."

Jim and Lynn sat quietly and waited.

Plunging ahead, Claire explained, "I feel like I should know what it is, but I can't put my finger on it. It's just out of reach, frustrating me to no end."

She glanced across at Jim, tapped her fingertips on the table, lowered her head, and fell quiet.

The three of them sat in silence once again until Jim cleared his throat and spoke up, "Actually, Claire, I was thinking the same thing. Have been since earlier today but I can't figure out what it is either."

"Maybe it will come through during the séance," Lynn suggested.

Claire concentrated on the coffee cup again and remarked suddenly, "I think it has something to do with the description of the perpetrator."

Jim's cup was halfway to his mouth when she made this pronouncement. Stopping, he put his coffee back on the table and gaped at her. "I've been having the same thoughts!"

Lynn watched them both and said encouragingly, "Go on…talk about it…it might help if you compare notes. What is it that's bothering you?" She waited and watched.

Claire started out slowly, "Well, I have the feeling that I already know this guy."

She stopped as if thinking through what she wanted to say next.

"I haven't seen a picture of him yet, but that's just the feeling I have…that I should know him…," her voice trailed off while considering the importance of what she had just said.

"Can you come up with any distinguishing characteristics? Do you see anything at all that has to do with his appearance?" Jim leaned in closer to the table and stared, waiting for Claire to respond.

After several agonizing seconds, she just shook her head, "No, nothing that just jumps out at me."

Jim sighed and took another drink of his coffee, savoring the hot liquid as it soothingly passed through his sore ribs.

Impulsively he spoke up, "I'm thinking it has something to do with the last time I was here, Lynn."

She raised her eyebrows in surprise.

"I remember you telling me something about the guy that faked his own death in the fire several years ago. Remember that?"

Nodding, she indicated that he should continue.

"Well, I was thinking of that case earlier today when I was explaining to Claire about how you might be able to help us."

"And…?" Lynn looked at him curiously.

"At that time you explained to me that the man was still alive but that the picture you were seeing was murky. You couldn't make out any definitive physical details and therefore you couldn't see where he might be."

Lynn grew excited and replied, "Yes, I remember now. I knew he was still alive but I couldn't make out his face."

"Do you remember why you couldn't see him clearly?" Jim waited breathlessly for her response.

"Yes, as a matter of fact I do. I sometimes get obscure images and they're due to a variety of reasons."

"Like what?" Claire asked, interrupting Lynn, budding interest showing on her face.

"Sometimes I can't see obvious features because the spirits themselves are not emanating enough energy to materialize."

"But," Jim interjected, "You told me the guy was still alive."

"Yes, yes Jim I remember, but that wasn't the case in the particular incident you were speaking about," Lynn chided him. "Claire wanted to know why I might have obstructed views of people during visions and I was giving her some of the reasons."

"Okay, I'm sorry."

Lynn smiled at him and took his hand, "Follow me and let's see if we can find out why you think it might have something to do with Libby's murder."

Claire flinched inwardly at the still-dawning reality of the statement.

Lynn picked up where she had left off, "Sometimes the image is unclear due to the very nature of the individual."

Jim frowned and asked, "What do you mean by that?"

"I mean that sometimes I don't get a very good picture of a person because he or she might look so much like everyone else that it is hard to see any distinguishing characteristics. Or...," she hesitated.

"Or what, Lynn?" Jim looked at her expectantly.

Talking low, she responded, "It's possible that the person could be disguising his or her identity."

Jim removed his hand from Lynn's and slapped it hard on the table, "That's what I was trying to remember! You told me that and I had a picture in my mind of him physically disguising himself!"

"And that's why it was so hard for me to see where he was at that time," Lynn explained further. "If he was deliberately changing his identity, it would be difficult to determine his whereabouts as well."

Claire remained unsettlingly quiet during this exchange, watching the two closely but not intruding into the conversation. Finally she asked, "What do you think this revelation has to do with Libby's...case?"

She couldn't bring herself to use the word 'murder' just yet even though she now grudgingly admitted to herself that it was true.

Why did I allow myself to get so personally involved! That's what I was taught from day one—don't get involved!

"It's very possible that Libby's killer is doing the same thing--intentionally hiding his identity through a variety of disguises," Jim explained.

Claire stared intently and questioned him, "Do you think we might already know the person responsible for whatever happened to Libby?"

Jim gazed back at her for what seemed like an eternity before replying, "I don't know, Claire, but I hope she plans to share that with us tonight."

CHAPTER TWENTY-ONE

"A dead man, what do you mean?" Clark Tomlinson gaped uncomprehendingly at Chief Hennessey.

"The fingerprints belong to a man who has already been declared legally dead," he explained. Marvin rapidly read through the information on the computer screen.

George Stanley read the same information and remarked, "I wonder how many identities this guy took on after he supposedly died." He shook his head in disgust.

"One thing's for sure, George, Mary's not going to keep my dinner warm."

Laughing, he responded, "Do you want me to give her a call and explain your absence on the first day of your retirement…save you from getting too much flak."

"I appreciate it, buddy, but that's my job. Your job is to start working backwards on Trent Newman until we find out where he's been since he 'died' and what identities he's been using in the meantime."

Officer Tomlinson continued to watch the interplay between the two senior officers before offering "Is there anything I can do to help?"

"You can help me, Clark," George replied, "I defer to your experience on computers and I'm sure you can speed the process along for us."

"No problem, sir," he answered, "I'll get started right away." Clark left the two men standing in front of the screen to answer the phone which was ringing in the background.

Chief stood in front of the desk, mesmerized by the information on the computer, "I'm still puzzled by one thing, George."

"What's that, Marvin?"

Chief Hennessey thought about the ramifications before replying, "Why did this guy put down Claire's name on his resume as a character reference?"

Officer Stanley just gazed at the screen in response. He started to answer but was interrupted by Clark Tomlinson. "Didn't you two just come back from Landry Trucking off highway 46?"

Marvin and George stared at him curiously before nodding in agreement.

"Did you talk to a man named Art Cane who works there?"

Again, the two nodded in unison.

"Well, his wife is on the phone and he hasn't come home yet. She tried calling and no one answered at the office. She called us because she was afraid he might have been involved in an accident on his way home, and the sheriff had already told her there were no accidents reported in his jurisdiction."

The two superior officers looked at each other.

"Ordinarily I would just tell her to wait until later before worrying, but since you were there today, I thought one of you might want to talk to her first."

George pushed by Clark and quickly picked up the phone. He introduced himself and asked Mrs. Cane what he could do for her.

Listening to her story, he got a sick feeling in his stomach when he realized that her husband was a man of strict habits—he woke up at the same time every day, ate breakfast, went to work, arriving at 8:00 a.m. sharp, and never went anywhere after work without first calling his wife. Alarm bells started going off but he assured Mrs. Cane that they would check at the office and let her know as soon as they could.

Hanging up the phone, he glanced over and saw both Chief Hennessey and Officer Tomlinson staring at him.

"Something tells me this isn't good."

"Do you want me to dispatch an officer to Landry Trucking?" Clark Tomlinson asked and waited for an answer.

"No, Clark, let us handle it. Chief and I will go to the trucking company and check it out, but you can help us by continuing to dig into Trent Newman's past—also delve into the dead man's past and try to come up with more information that will tie the two together. It looks like they are one and the same since their fingerprints match, but we will still need all the evidence we can get our hands on to link them."

Marvin grabbed his Glock, 9mm. and badge off his desk before walking out to a patrol car with George.

"You only <u>thought</u> you were done with those"

"Yeah and something tells me this is going to be a long night."

In the small house in the middle of the woods, candlelight flickered in the front window, illuminating the darkness only enough for three shadowy figures to be seen seated around a table.

"To our higher being, the one we call our God, I offer a prayer that You protect us from evil spirits. Do not allow them to come in; only allow those, whom we want to communicate with, to join us," Lynn spoke aloud with hands open-palmed, lying flat on the table.

Claire and Jim sat on either side of her, their hands open too, resting gently on the table. They remained as still and quiet as possible, but both fought the urge to shift uncomfortably in their chairs, a reaction to the unfamiliar situation and the prayer recited by Lynn.

After several minutes of silence, Claire glanced over at Lynn and watched as her fingers started to move, first slowly, and then picking up speed, drumming a rhythm against the tabletop. Jim noticed the movement too and looked in astonishment as she raised her hands off the table and began making movements in the air.

They sat hushed as Lynn's fingers flew. Finally Claire reacted and said, "Slow down, Libby, or better yet, can you talk to us while you sign?"

Jim just stared at Claire, amazed at her quick reaction and understanding.

Through Lynn, Libby responded in a halting, almost child-like voice, slightly nasal in quality, "Yes, I am Libby."

"We are here to help you. What do you want from us?" Jim asked earnestly.

"Find me," Lynn made the sign for 'find' and pointed to her chest to indicate she was talking in the first person.

"Where are you, Libby?" Jim and Claire both spoke in unison.

Fingers flew as the answer appeared.

Jim put up his hand and requested, "Please slow down. Tell us where you are."

Again, fingers spelled out an answer to the question.

"P-i-n-e L-a-k-e, Pine Lake?" Jim asked intently.

"Pine Lake," Libby meekly responded.

"Are you buried there?" Claire leaned forward, eagerly awaiting her reply.

Lynn's hand went up and down in a movement for the word 'yes'.

Saddened, Claire put her head down. Jim took her hand in his and said, "I promise you, Libby. We'll find you."

Relieved, Lynn's face took on a more youthful and happy countenance, and then immediately clouded up and changed once again. Hurriedly and in a hushed tone she said, "Be careful. My killer is watching."

Claire and Jim looked at each other, unsure what to do next.

Finally Claire spoke up, "Who is your killer, Libby? Is it Trent?"

Lynn gazed at her for the longest time before she finally signed and said, "Your friend."

"What do you mean by that, Libby?" Claire stared at Lynn, confused.

"Your friend," she replied, "He's your friend. You know him."

Claire gasped, "My friend? I know him? Who is it, Libby?"

She sighed and said again, "Your friend. You will remember when you see him." Her voice sounded far away, "You know him..."

Agitatedly Lynn started to squirm in her chair and then went limp.

Jim and Claire watched her intensely until she began to move and opened her eyes. She looked confused and exhausted, but managed to pull herself up straighter in the chair as she whispered, "Did Libby come? Did you get a chance to talk to her?"

Claire and Jim sat there, unable to move, unable to talk, shocked at the realization that the killer was known to one of them and he had been watching.

As all good troopers are trained to do, Captain Hennessey and Corporal Stanley took in the surroundings at the trucking company lot as they drove in. No trucks idling; no drivers standing around; only nightfall coming in fast, hiding any other details that might prove activity in an otherwise deserted parking lot. Both of them glanced at the office and noted that no lights were shining and the 'Closed' sign was displayed on the front door. After they pulled into a space in front of the office, George instinctively pulled his gun out of his shoulder harness while exiting the car. Marvin did the same. Even though neither man noticed any movement in the office, Chief motioned for George to go around to the back of the building and check any other doors and windows.

After stationing himself by the southwest corner where he could keep an eye on anyone trying to escape out the back door or window, George motioned to Marvin that he was in place. Captain Hennessey approached the front door and knocked, while proclaiming, "Police! This is the state police! Open the door!"

Both men waited breathlessly but to no avail. No movement came from the building. No figures were sighted inside. Silence was the only reply. After several minutes and two more announcements with no response, Marvin tried the front door and found it locked. "Try the back door, George."

Chief waited for a reply from him and then peered around the corner in time to see George shaking his head negatively.

"Look in the window," Marvin mouthed as he pointed in that direction.

While George was checking the lone back window, Captain Hennessey shaded his eyes and scrutinized the inside of the office earnestly. He allowed his vision to adjust to the dark as he gazed around the interior of the room. Even though his training had prepared him for any sudden movement, he was still startled when George came around the corner and approached him. He exhaled quickly and asked, "Didn't see anything?"

"Not sure, but I think I might have," George replied cautiously.

"I'm going to get the flashlight out of the car," he continued as he walked to the patrol car.

Watching him grab the flashlight out of the glove compartment, Marvin raised his eyebrows and, out of curiosity, followed him around to the back of the building.

George shone the light in the window and scanned the room, carefully illuminating one small space at a time.

His movements became more deliberate and slow as the light approached a cramped area back by a sink next to a long table. Only one corner of the table was visible through the window.

"Look closely, Marvin. I thought I saw something poking out by that table leg." He trained the light on the leg and the floor surrounding it. "There! See it?"

Marvin peered through the back door and said in response, "Looks like part of a shoe sticking out under that table to me. That's what I think. What about you?"

George nodded and said, "And that gives us plenty of right to enter."

He put his shoulder into the door and shoved hard. The age and condition of the door didn't deter the two men and it easily gave way with just one push.

George regained his balance and entered the office ahead of Chief. He flipped the light switch on and quickly surveyed the interior to ensure that no one was hiding inside.

With guns drawn, both officers combed the small office, checking every nook and cranny, before putting their full attention on the body lying on the floor under the table.

"Looks like Art Cane won't be coming home tonight...or any night," Marvin quietly observed.

George holstered his Glock and walked toward the front of the office. "I'll call and get our guys out here. You secure the area and take notes."

He added, "You might use your cell phone to call <u>your</u> wife. I'm sure she wants to know that you're coming home...just not anytime soon."

Marvin continued to stare down at Art Cain. He knew he needed to call Mary, but he was bothered by the fact that there was one more person he needed to call, Claire Dungarven. Because if he was right, she needed that phone call a lot more than Mary did.

Claire and Jim sat in the car in front of Lynn's house, pondering all the new information from the séance and the implications.

"So what do we do now?" Claire started the car and looked over at Jim, concern written all over her face.

He grimaced, more out of pain than indecision, and said, "Well, we need to go out to Pine Lake and see if we can find the gravesite, but..." He touched the place on his head where he had the stitches and shifted in his seat.

Claire glanced over at him as she pulled away from the parking spot. *He's not looking too good. What an idiot I've been! I picked him up from the hospital and have had him out all day today...and for what? To chase a ghost?*

Claire winced, *He needs to be in bed, resting, recovering from his injuries.*

"Jim, I'm taking you home with me," she spoke up impetuously.

He started to put up his hand to object, but she persisted, "No, you need to rest."

Adding, "Besides, what could we see tonight? We should wait until morning."

If you're feeling well enough, she added to herself. *If not, I'll go by myself.*

Jim gazed at her for the longest time, not sure if he should trust her, but finally the pain made him give in to her insistence. "Okay, but promise me you'll not do anything stupid."

"Whatever do you mean?" She looked at him coyly.

If she only knew how cute she looks right now!

Sternly, he said, "You know perfectly well what I mean."

She grinned at him and responded, "Of course, I'll not go without you."

He stared at her warily but nodded his head and said, "I trust you on this one, Claire, but don't let me down."

He stopped talking as he remembered something she'd said, "And, by the way, did you say 'I'm taking you home with me' or was that wishful thinking on my part?"

She winked at him and smiled, "How could I ever let you down."

He grinned and chided her, "You're avoiding my question."

"No, I'm not!"

Jim's smile widened as he waited, not saying anything.

She sighed, "Okay, it wasn't wishful thinking...but don't get your hopes up for anything more than my playing 'Florence Nightingale' until you're feeling better."

He laughed and said, "Alright, I can accept that...especially the last part."

Confused, she looked across the seat at him and asked, "What last part?"

Devilishly he replied, "The part about 'until I'm feeling better'. It gives me something to look forward to."

"See, you're feeling better already," she batted her eyelashes at him and took his hand, grasping it tightly in hers.

Jim leaned closer and looked her in the eye. He watched her for any sign that she might be considering trying something on her own. They were being playful with each other...*and it turns me on!* But, he didn't see any telltale signs that she was lying to him.

Timidly at first, and then more urgently, he kissed her on the lips. Her response was warm, tempting, desiring and desirable.

Then her lips moved up the side of his face and very gently caressed his stitches.

He pulled her hand up to his mouth and kissed each finger, lovingly staring at her the whole time.

Reluctantly, they pulled apart, their eyes met, and the impulse to not stop was evident on both of their faces.

But the beginning of a headache drummed through his head, forcing him to lean back against the seat and close his eyes. The pain grudgingly forced him to accept her promise. He was convinced that he had a solid commitment from her not to put herself in any danger.

Unfortunately, he didn't see the subtle movement of her left hand as she took it off the steering wheel, rested it against the driver's door, and crossed her fingers.

CHAPTER TWENTY-TWO

"Huh, that's strange. She's not home," Marvin Hennessey allowed the phone to ring until voice mail took over. "Claire, call me when you get this," he gruffly spoke into the phone and hung up.

Distracted by the arrival of more officers and in a rush to secure the crime scene, he forgot to mention that he was calling from his cell phone, and to tell her the significance of his call. It would be hours later before he realized that she had not called him back.

But in the meantime, there were duties to perform. George Stanley was perfectly capable of leading the investigation, but Chief felt a certain responsibility since he had been the one to contact Art Cane in the first place. A brief wave of guilt came over him at the thought that Mr. Cane might have lost his life due to their conversation this afternoon, but he quickly shook the feeling off. He had to put on his professional demeanor and begin the laborious process of collecting evidence.

George came up and stood beside Marvin. "Looks like he was stabbed as he was trying to run away from the killer."

Chief nodded in agreement and added, "From where the body is located, I would suspect that he fell while running towards the back door, trying to escape."

"There's a severe gash on the victim's head," one of the patrolmen observed. "He might have hit his head on the table when he fell."

"The knife wound was what killed him though," George muttered gruffly.

The forensic investigator said, "Yes, even though he lost a lot of blood from the head injury, it was secondary to the stabbing...right through the heart. The perp must have come up from behind, put him in a head lock, and stabbed him. He knew what he was doing." Adding, "Did you find the knife?"

Both George and Marvin shook their heads and said, "No."

George suggested, "He probably took the weapon with him, but I'll have some of the men check around the office and in the parking lot in hopes we get lucky and find it close by."

Marvin snorted, "Don't get your hopes up, George. He's too smart for that, and you and I know it."

"Yeah," he considered, putting his head down before continuing, "Are you thinking what I'm thinking...that Trent Newman did this?"

"Right now he's our number one suspect as far as I'm concerned...but we have to find him first."

"And, we need to send an officer out to let Mrs. Cane know." George reminded him. His mind was running through all the procedures that needed to be accomplished at the scene.

"I'll ask Clark to send someone out...and while I'm at it, I'll check on his progress with the background check."

Hours later, after the sheriff's deputy had come out to take a report and lift some fingerprints found in the house, Claire was still picking up the clutter left by the intruder. She had to grin when she remembered how embarrassed Jim had been when his chief deputy, Rusty Timmons, had needled him unmercifully about staying with Claire. The two men enjoyed a joking exchange that left Jim on the receiving end for most of the conversation. She was sure that it wouldn't be long before the whole Conservancy police force knew about their budding relationship.

But, I don't care! It's kind of nice to think about it.

After Rusty left, Claire put Jim to bed in her spare bedroom over his protests that she needed his help in cleaning up the house. She insisted that he could use the rest more than she needed the help and he finally acquiesced, took more pain medication, and fell asleep shortly after his head hit the pillow.

Smiling, she thought about how important Jim was becoming in her life. *How come I didn't meet him earlier*, she wondered.

Problem is I wouldn't have been any more ready to get serious, even with Jim. She folded items and put them back in her dresser. *Just like Doug, I would have put my career first. It was always like that.* She contemplated what her life would have been like if she had married.

Greg was the one who touched my heart, though. I didn't know him long but there was something about him that just made me melt. Besides those gorgeous eyes, she remembered, *he had the most charismatic personality. He could charm any woman...and he did*, she scoffed at herself. *How could I have been so stupid!* She closed the drawer and sighed, *well, at least I had the courage to walk away from that relationship when I saw him with his wife. What a slime! He sure had me fooled!*

Claire carefully smoothed out the bed where the clothing had been piled up and yawning she realized how tired she felt.

Grabbing her nightgown out of the closet, she proceeded to undress and continued reminiscing, *Jim is everything I've been looking for in a man. Greg couldn't hold a candle to him! Jim's smart, sexy, sweet...all the qualities I need. Why waste my time wondering why he didn't come into my life sooner. He's here now and I plan to hold on to this one. He's a keeper.*

Turning down the bedspread, Claire shuddered in pleasure when she thought about how close he was and how fortunate she was to have him. *Yes, I'm one lucky gal*, she smiled as she pulled up the sheet and blanket.

In her rush to clean up the house, and with exhaustion quickly settling in, she didn't think to check the phone for messages. But even if she had, she might not have been concerned about any urgency to call Chief back. She drifted off to sleep unaware that a murder had occurred...and as a result of that crime, her own life was in more danger than she could ever imagine.

The moon hung in the night sky, almost full, its outline edge-straight and stark against the black surroundings. Stars blinked around it but they only served as a minor distraction from the magnificence of the moon in all its glory. Tomorrow night it would be full, no edges, a luminous ring of blazing light to ignite the darkness...and make apparitions more visible in our earthly world.

One spirit in particular was anticipating that full moon. Libby had been waiting, and watching, for a long time. She stood by Claire's bed and gazed down at her in wonderment. *The time has finally come! She'll find me and bring peace of mind to my family and friends. She's my savior!*

Claire shifted in her bed. She sensed the cold and intuitively pulled the blanket up under her chin.

I need to protect her though, because <u>he</u> plans to follow her! Fear gripped Libby, and as a result, her energy weakened. If anyone present in the house had been awake, that person would have noticed a dimming of the outline, slowly fading away, and simultaneously, a gradual rise in room temperature. But no one was awake and Libby realized that she would have to invade Claire's dreams one more time to warn her of the danger that awaited her tomorrow.

Quickening warmth invaded the bedroom and Claire felt the tense relaxation that exhaustion carries with it. As she routinely passed from REM sleep into a deeper realm...the kind that brings dreams that don't make sense in the morning...or, that are not remembered in the calm of a new dawn...she was peacefully unaware of what tonight and tomorrow night would bring.

CHAPTER TWENTY-THREE

"Thanks, Clark. Send Ralston. He's very good at these kinds of things. He'll know what to say to Mrs. Cane."

Marvin listened on his cell phone as Trooper Tomlinson talked.

"Yeah, we're still working the scene…and will be overnight…but he definitely was murdered. Sheriff's department is working with us on this one, so we should have plenty of manpower to cover all aspects of the investigation."

Again Chief listened as Clark asked him about what to tell Mrs. Cane.

"She'll need to know that he was killed…and Detective Trooper Ralston might want to ask her if she knows anyone who might have a motive…," pausing as Clark Tomlinson spoke. "No, we're not ready to talk to the media yet. If anyone finds out and calls, take their number and we'll get back with them, but we don't want them showing up here just yet."

Changing the subject, "By the way, did you have time to find out any more about Trent Newman's background?"

Marvin's eyes lit up, "Oh really! Well, that's interesting."

"Uh huh," His eyebrows knitted together in worry. "Well, keep digging. I think we'll find the connections. If not, we've got the fingerprints and they match. We can also use any circumstantial evidence and the timeline to prove that the two identities are the same."

He paused as an idea struck him. "Why don't you go ahead and start working backwards using the dead guy's identity. Interview friends, find out what you can about him from the crime file, and get back with me as soon as you locate anything of interest."

George came up to Marvin. "Look, Clark, I gotta go but call me. Yeah, thanks. Bye."

"What did he say? Is he going to get someone to go out to the house?"

"Yes, and he had some interesting conclusions to share with me about Trent Newman."

"Why, what'd he say?"

"He thinks we can use more than the prints to prove that Trent Newman and the other man are one and the same…the timeline. The guy dies suspiciously and then all of a sudden Trent appears."

"Did Clark talk to the man's wife yet?"

"No, that's the 'interesting part'," Chief paused as George stared at him, "The wife disappeared right after she declared him dead. No one's seen her, knows where she is, and it's like she vanished off the face of the earth."

The two men stood facing each other, heads down.

Finally Marvin spoke up, "I suggested he work backwards on the dead guy and see what he can come up with there. Maybe there'll be other indications in his past that he was leading more than one life."

"Good idea."

Sighing, "Yeah but I hope he can tell us more than just that he had a penchant for taking on different identities and killing."

"What's that?"

"I'm hoping he can find something that will tell us how Claire Dungarven fits into his past."

Claire stirred in her sleep as images swiftly flitted across her dreams, like a fast-moving, brightly-colored kaleidoscope. She saw Libby; she was dressed all in white; the snowy background made it hard to distinguish her small, fragile frame from the bare trees which provided the only other details that stood out in her dream.

Then, bright crimson blood drops started dripping from her fingers. They stained the snow as quickly as they fell, forming clots of red, growing larger and larger, mixing with the snow, diluting, until becoming a shimmery liquid pool. Claire squirmed at the vision, uncomfortable with what it symbolized, because she realized that she was looking at Libby's burial site.

Her movements in bed became more restless as the fluid started to bubble up, turning the white surrounding snow into the same vibrant red liquid, oozing from the ground, growing, conquering the beautiful white winter wonderland until all that was left was ugly and foreboding.

Libby put her hands together in the same gesture she had shown Claire before, *Help*. She repeated the gesture and pointed to her chest, signing *Help me*. Standing in the middle of the rusty red muck, she started to sink. Quicksand-like in texture, it was consuming her at a frightening pace.

Helplessly, Claire watched as the rose tattoo on Libby's ankle disappeared in the abyss first. She let out a small, almost silent cry as Libby's legs vanished in the liquid, then her hips, as the onslaught continued, marching up to engulf her torso, her neck, and finally her face. Horrified, Claire let out a series of soft mewing sounds, kicking at her covers as the scarlet mud devoured Libby, but not before capturing the absolutely terrifying panic in her eyes. It was a look that would haunt Claire for the rest of her life.

The investigation into the death of Art Cane at the Landry Trucking Company office lasted until the first rays of sunrise could be seen hovering over the horizon, ready to announce the beginning of another day in all its blazing glory. Due to the warming temperature, fog was projected to hang around until midmorning and this would stunt the impact of the always beautiful sunrise. In time, it promised to dissipate and let the sun have its day.

The anticipated warm weather that the forecasters had predicted earlier in the week was finally arriving. It prefaced a melting of the ice and snow cover that had hung around the vicinity for the last few days.

People living in southern Indiana were pleased to see this much-needed break in the temperature. Roads were still covered with dangerous patches of ice that had left well-worn ruts, difficult to transverse, often ending in tracks that foretold of slide-offs on the sides of the roads.

Marvin Hennessey looked up at the morning sky and heaved a sigh of relief, *maybe by the time I wake up this afternoon, I can look forward to walking down to get the mail without the fear of falling on the ice!* He could only hope that Mary would feel sorry for him and let him sleep that long. *If not, it'll be a long day.*

He tried unsuccessfully to stifle a yawn and thought, *I should probably check in at the office first and see if Clark left anything for me.*

The second time it happened, he couldn't stop the yawn. *I'm not as young as I used to be. These all-nighters take their toll on me now.*

He smiled at a thought, *I'm supposed to be retired and yet still worried about how I'm going solve this crime!*

He got in the patrol car and felt the weariness overtake him. *But, if I'm going to be involved in the case, I need to go home and get some sleep...or I won't be worth much to anybody!*

He started the car. *Plus, I owe it to Mary to go home and explain what's happening. She's probably sitting at the kitchen table right now, sipping her coffee...and stewing!* He chuckled at the picture that his mind's eye conjured up for him. *Nope, she won't be happy.*

He knew that there was something else tugging at the perimeter of his brain, but exhaustion was keeping it a secret, and as the tiredness invaded his body at break-neck speed, he couldn't for the life of him remember what it was.

I'll remember this afternoon...nothing is too important that it can't wait a half-day longer.

CHAPTER TWENTY-FOUR

Pacing around the kitchen, Claire tried to keep busy by continuing to put items away that were strewn all over the countertops. *Boy, whoever did this sure made a mess! I'm going to be busy cleaning up for while.*

She stopped, holding a washcloth in midair, and focused on the disturbing dream she had had. *Libby's waiting for us to come and find her...and I'm worried about putting things away!*

She turned and walked down the hall towards the bedrooms. Standing in front of the room Jim was in, she pushed the door open quietly and looked in. He was sleeping peacefully and she was grateful for that. *He needs his sleep. Better leave him alone.*

Claire gently closed the door and stood there for a few more seconds, conflicted about what to do next. She felt an urgency to go out to Pine Lake but knew that Jim wanted to come with her.

He made me promise...but I knew last night that it would be difficult to keep a promise. She bowed her head. *I just don't know what to do. Should I wait for him to wake up, should I wake him up, or should I go by myself?*

She turned and headed back down the hall.

In the kitchen Claire recalled the ghastly dream and how it had awakened her at the ungodly hour of 5:00 a.m. *It was so real!*

Recalling how terrified Libby looked, Claire tried to fight off the tears, but they started to spill from her eyes, and she swiped at them before they threatened to run down her cheeks. *That young woman deserves some peace! We need to find her body!*

She headed towards her bedroom to make the bed. Claire wanted to be ready to leave as soon as Jim woke up.

Hurriedly pulling up the covers and placing the pillows on the bed, she had time to think about the urgency of the situation. *I can't wait for Jim! I need to get out there NOW!*

She went into the bathroom to brush her hair…and stopped while holding the brush mid-air. *I have to handle this without Jim.*

She winced at the thought of how angry he would be.

But, he'll just have to be mad because, I'm not going to wake him up!

In the spare bedroom Jim slept, unaware of what Claire was thinking at that moment. If he had been aware of the conflict going on in her head, he would have immediately jumped out of bed and joined her in the search for Libby's grave. But, Claire made a decision to let him sleep…and it was one that could cost her her life.

When Marvin Hennessey arrived home that morning, Mary was waiting for him. She had been married to him for 37 years and she understood a life spent in law enforcement. She didn't ask any questions but let him unwind, fed him breakfast, and watched as he headed towards the bedroom to catch a well-deserved nap. She knew he would probably be up before he had a full eight hours of sleep, but she didn't remind him of that; she just gave him a kiss and sent him on his way.

But she did intend to protect him…as she had so many times in the past. If anyone called and needed to speak to him before he was up, she would politely but firmly tell them to call back or she would take a message for him and he could call that person later. She didn't sway on that point. He was her man and she would run interference for him! That was the way it had been all these years, and that would be the way she would handle it this time. *After all,* she reasoned, *he's retired.*

He's retired? Yeah, right…I'll believe that when we've had a few weeks of no business phone calls, no unexpected trips to the office, just blissful and uneventful boredom!

She almost laughed out loud at that thought though. She wasn't being sarcastic, only realistic. *It will be hard for Marvin…being 'retired'… but we'll give it our best shot.*

❖

At the State Police post, Clark Tomlinson was pouring over the computer, trying to make sense of the information he was reading. *This man is an enigma! He was a loner...and that fits with Trent Newman's profile. He lived in Brown County, in fact he lived in Sweetwater. Hmmm. Wonder if he knew Claire from there?* Then he remembered, *No, she didn't move down there until recently.*

Clark continued to study the facts he had from both crime files and suddenly his eyes lit on one fact that had eluded them before. *Bingo! They both worked as truckers. Now we're getting somewhere. This is too coincidental for it not to have a bearing on the cases. Hmmm. This guy worked for a company out of Tennessee.*

Picking up the phone, he decided to call there first. It was still early in the morning but fortunately he finally got through to the personnel director...and what he told Trooper Tomlinson was very interesting. Clark followed it up with a call to Landry's main office. It suggested some intriguing new possibilities.

He had to get in touch with Chief Hennessey right away. He picked up the phone again and dialed his cell phone. *I'll leave a message for him if he doesn't pick up right away. I'm pretty sure he's out at the scene. I know the others are still there. But, if I don't hear from him soon, I'll call his home.*

Clark waited until he heard Chief's voice mail come on; he left a message and hung up. Looking at the clock he realized that his shift was almost over and decided to leave a message for George Stanley so that he could be filled in too. *I know he'll stop in before going home. I'm sure there will be evidence that he needs to drop off since he is the lead investigator on the murder investigation. That way if Chief doesn't call back in the next fifteen minutes, when I go home, George can see my message and let Chief know too.*

His shift ended and Clark Tomlinson left for home. The message he left for George contained the interesting new information. When Officer Stanley returned from the trucking company office, he would be astonished at what it told him and the conclusion Claire came to.

I'VE FOUND THE LINK!

Jim Hoppes woke up around noon. Still groggy from sleep and feeling the effects of several broken ribs and twelve stitches in his head, it took him a while to realize where he was and whose bed he was sleeping in. Even through the pain he smiled at the thought and lay there for a few more minutes, relishing in the fact that he was so fortunate to have someone like Claire in his life right now.

More out of sorrow and not pain, he winced when he remembered back to the last time he felt such happiness. He was newly graduated from the Police Academy and engaged to Marty. She had been the love of his life since high school. They planned to wed and settle down after he got a job. Tragically he would not feel the euphoria of marrying his first love…and would not feel the same kind of love for another female until he met Claire again.

Marty had been going through her training to become a member of the Fire Department in Darwin Township in Indianapolis at the same time Jim was completing his training at the Police Academy. She graduated and started working at almost the same time Jim got a job with Lakeland Township on the west side of Indianapolis. Only two weeks on the job, she was walking across the street, returning to the fire station with lunch from a nearby restaurant, when a car came out of nowhere and hit her, knocking her onto the hood and into the street.

By the time Jim arrived at the hospital, Marty was already in surgery. She had a blood clot on the brain that was causing her brain to swell. The surgery was a success but she was in a coma and remained in a coma for the rest of her time on earth. Two months later she died and Jim had been grief-stricken ever since. He never remarried and had little interest in dating other women even though he tried.

Plenty of women were interested, but it just didn't seem right to me. The hurt over losing Marty was too strong.

Eventually Jim knew that the best thing for him to do was move forward and he applied for the job as the Sheriff's Deputy in charge of Sweetwater Conservancy.

Not exactly a great place to meet women! Too isolated. But that's what I wanted at the time...just to live my life and keep Marty in my memories.

He had been here ever since and had settled into a normal routine. *As normal as I could make it...*

He sighed heavily. *I miss her so much!*

Then, he remembered where he was and his thoughts turned to Claire. *She came into my life just in the nick of time. Call it midlife crisis or whatever, but I was really beginning to wonder if I could find someone to share my life with again.*

He smiled. *She's beautiful and I can't believe my luck!*

Jim settled his head deeper in the pillow. *Her eyes, her face, her legs...everything about her is gorgeous! And, best of all, she cares for me too. I can tell in the way she kissed me.*

I can't wait to tell her how I feel, he thought as he gingerly sat up and swung his feet over the side of the bed. He exited the bedroom, feeling refreshed and rejuvenated, ready to face the day.

As he walked down the hall towards the kitchen and living room area, he slowed his pace as he realized how quiet the house was. "Claire...where are you?"

He continued down the hall until he arrived at the end and peeked around the corner into the kitchen. "Claire?"

Huh, that's funny. She's not here. Cell phone's on the table. Maybe she's still in bed. Grinning, he was tempted by the possibility of that being true and what he might do if she <u>was</u> still in bed.

But, when he looked in her bedroom and saw the bed made, Jim started to get a queasy feeling in his stomach. *She wouldn't go without me! She promised me that she would wait!*

But as the alarming reality set in that she was not there, he quickly ran to the window and looked out.

No Claire, but what he saw in the yard almost caused his heart to stop. There standing in the same place where the blood, the water and the rose had been was the faint apparition of Libby Newman. She looked at him with the most profound sadness and motioned as if she wanted him to come to her. The lingering morning fog clung to the surroundings and hampered his view but it was Libby. He stared at her for a few seconds and then she faded away. He quickly looked around to see if anyone might have seen her but no one else was watching from a window but Jim. No one saw her and Jim knew in a heartbeat what her message was to him.

Find Claire and you'll find me…and my killer.

CHAPTER TWENTY-FIVE

While riding back to the state police post with one of the troopers, George Stanley went over the known facts about the death of Art Cane.

He was by himself when the perpetrator entered the office. No witnesses have surfaced to dispute that. The office is in an isolated area and even though we will put out a request for information, there probably weren't any other people in the area at the time the crime was committed, or they would have called already.

It looks like he was running from his attacker but there were no signs of a struggle; everything was in order. The victim was caught by surprise. He tried to escape but didn't get far. The person who killed him came up from behind and stabbed him in the heart. No blood spatters were in any other part of the office. He dropped right where he was standing beside the table, and died almost instantly.

Fingerprints from the scene might yield some more clues, but without the weapon, we're at a real disadvantage. There's likely to be a lot of fingerprints in the office; most of them will be people who work there, including Trent Newman.

George felt the car slow down as the driver focused on the road ahead. The fog was hampering his ability to see clearly.

DNA might yield some blood that doesn't belong to the victim. It will take some time before we have the results due to the backlog at the lab. And then, if there is DNA that doesn't match Art Cane, we'll have to have probable cause to collect a sample from Mr. Newman.

Officer Stanley shook his head dejectedly when considering the time required for any results to come back.

The frustrating part is the waiting, he thought. *It could be months before we know for sure if there is other DNA...and then we would have to convince Trent Newman to supply us with a specimen...or try to get one ourselves.*

He sighed knowingly at the realization that this case could occupy his mind for the next several months.

Sure hate the thought that Chief will be involved with the investigation. He was so looking forward to his retirement.

George smiled. *I guess it'll be put on hold for now.*

He glanced up in surprise when he realized that they had already arrived back at the post.

I'll just go in and drop off what I have and go home!

Suddenly recognizing how tired he was, George yawned and rubbed his eyes.

He walked into the building and acknowledged some of the staff with a wave before arriving at his desk. He put the crime evidence in his file basket as his attention was drawn to a note left on the desk.

Raising his eyebrows, he recognized the seriousness of the information that Clark had shared.

If he's right and we've found a link, we have a possible serial killer on our hands.

After assigning a variety of duties to some of the shift personnel present in the office, George Stanley decided to call and see if Marvin had gone to bed yet. He wanted to get Clark's conclusions to him as soon as possible.

Mary answered the phone and told George, in no uncertain terms, that he was asleep and she would give him the message when he woke up.

He had to smile because he knew how protective Mary was and the tone of her voice indicated that she was a little irritated too.

I understand. After all, he's supposed to be retired! Of course that hasn't lasted one day yet!

George apologized and left a brief message to tell Chief when he woke up that the suspect they were checking on probably does have multiple identities and that it seemed to be confirmed by separate phone interviews with two different trucking companies.

George explained that Marvin would understand what he was talking about and he would fill him in on the details when he called back.

Mary relented a little and promised to let Marvin know as soon as he woke up.

After the conversation ended, George realized how tired he was and made preparations to go home himself and get some sleep.

He left the office feeling satisfied with the progress the investigation was taking so far and looking forward to a good sleep before returning the next day.

Claire drove to the Pine Lake vicinity cautiously and slowly. Remnants of the morning fog were still hanging in the air like a shroud, making driving difficult. But, she occupied her mind by remembering some of the landmarks, and they brought back good family memories.

Dad used to stop here at this little store and get his bait for fishing. I remember the man who owned it then would always give me a piece of that hard candy. What did they call it? Let me think. I know they still sell it at the Old Nashville Sweet Shop...horehound. That's what it was.

Or, if he was feeling really generous, I got one of those sugary orange slice candies. Those were my favorite! Dad used to laugh at me because I would make it last as long as I could, licking all the sugar off, chewing slowly, savoring the last bite for what seemed like hours before I swallowed it. Claire grinned at the memories.

Haven't been back in this location for several years. Last time I was here was probably ten years ago. It's really changed since then! More houses, more businesses. What a shame! It used to be such a beautiful area. Now it's occupied by buildings instead of trees! Well, that's progress I guess.

She frowned. *But that's why I moved down here...to get away from the downside of progress...and to enjoy nature.*

She brought her mind back to the present and looked around in time to notice that she had passed a familiar intersection. *Oops. I think that is where I was supposed to turn.*

She hastily wheeled around in a gas station parking lot and headed back towards the side road.

With all the changes in topography, it might be hard for me to locate the area that Libby showed me in my dream.

Claire glanced at the clock and realized that she might not have much time left before darkness settled in. Even though it was afternoon, due to the time change and shorter days, her search could last into nightfall.

I should have started earlier. I knew how long it would take to get here...but I couldn't make up my mind about leaving with or without Jim.

She remembered hearing Jim begin to stir and made a swift decision to leave before he woke up. She was so concerned about his injuries that she didn't want to put him in any more danger.

I've never felt like this before, she admitted. *He's such a wonderful guy and I need to pinch myself to believe that I might have found 'the one' at this time in my life!*

She felt the car sway and looked up in time to realize that she was driving too fast for the road conditions. She almost went into a spin when she hit a hard clump of ice. Luckily she did not overcorrect and had the car under control again in a few seconds.

Whoa! I'd better pay close attention to the road and not get lost in my thoughts again, or I'll wind up in the hospital like Jim!

Neither one of us would be of any use to Libby if that happened!

Claire focused all of her attention on the road and gradually made her way to the Pine Lake recreational area parking lot. She parked her car, stepped out, looked around, and tried to get her bearings.

As remote as it seemed in the vision, I'd better get my boots out of the trunk. It'll be muddy, snowy, sloppy, and tricky if I'm planning to hike for a while...and I think I will be. If I remember correctly, it's a ways from here, but I can't recall any other parking areas.

She hesitated, not sure if she should begin her search in the immediate area or not. Eventually she made a decision that would cause her search to last into dark.

I guess it's as good a place to start as any.

And with that, Claire prepared to hike the trails until she found what she was looking for.

In the background Marvin Hennessey faintly heard the persistent ringing of the telephone. After several rings, he was tempted to roll out of bed and get it himself until he groggily remembered that Mary was home and she would answer it.

As many years as we've been together, she'll wake me up if someone needs me.

After a few minutes of silence, he yawned and turned over to go back to sleep.

Must not be that important.

He quickly fell back to sleep, oblivious to the fact that Mary was deliberately not answering the phone.

Hmmm. Must not be home yet. Jim looked at the receiver, pondering what to do next. *I guess I could call Rusty and have him come over and take me home.*

Frowning, *I'd hoped to have Chief go with me to find Claire, but guess I'll need to do it on my own.*

He studied the phone and considered his options once more. *I left a message, so Marvin knows where I'll be…*

Urgently he radioed and requested that Rusty come and pick him up at Claire's house.

He wasn't sure but thought he could almost hear the teasing tone that Rusty tried to suppress in his most professional voice. "I'll be there in five."

Jim gathered up his jacket and wrote a quick note to Claire before Rusty arrived. He hoped that his instincts were wrong and that she would be home soon. On the off chance that he might be mistaken, he carefully worded it so that she would not become unduly alarmed.

On my way to Pine Lake. Called Chief and left a message for him to join us. Meet you there. Love, Jim.

Trent Newman rushed back to the Conservancy to keep tabs on Claire after completing his overnight assignment. With no sleep, he fought desperately against the drowsiness his body was experiencing, but his senses were startled awake when he drove up just in time to see Jim Hoppes exit her house and hop into a patrol car. Thrown off guard, he decided to follow the car at a discreet distance as it turned onto another street. *This must be where he lives.*

Trent slowed down to turn onto a side street, still within view, but unobtrusive to any witnesses. He watched as Jim waved goodbye to the officer in the police car and walked into his house. *Think I'll lay low for a while and see what he's planning to do.*

His eyebrows shot up when he saw Jim exit his house quickly and get into his car.

He seems to be in a hurry to get somewhere.

Making a snap decision to monitor Jim's whereabouts, Trent carefully stayed hidden until Jim turned on to the main road. Then, he pulled out and followed him. *Maybe he'll lead me to Claire.*

If so, I'll reveal my true identity to her...and get rid of Jim Hoppes. He grinned at the thought. *Then she'll be mine and mine alone. No one else can have her but me!*

Trent focused on the road ahead, but if anyone had seen his eyes, they would have remarked on the burning intensity that seemed to emanate from them. It could almost be described as rage. And if they had looked down, they would have been convinced. A glint of steel would have captured their attention and their own eyes would have widened in surprise and anguish as they realized that the steel belonged to a knife that was placed surreptitiously on the passenger seat.

Turning over in bed, Marvin Hennessey opened his eyes when the sunlight flooded his consciousness. Sighing restfully, he started to close his eyes again when he realized that if the sun was out, it must mean the fog had lifted and it was afternoon. He needed to wake up.

Still...he smiled at the thought that since he was retired he could stay in bed as long as he wanted. But then he remembered last night, and his professional obligations came flooding back into his memory like a waterfall cascading over a mountain. *I need to check with Mary and see if there are any messages.*

He yawned as he started moving towards the bathroom. *Better take a shower first or she won't even talk to me!*

Turning on the water, Chief stepped gingerly into the bathtub and let the hot blast of liquid force him awake with its soothing but potent outpouring. He heard Mary open the door while he was applying shampoo to his head.

"So, you're finally up," she joked.

"Yeah, I think so," he responded, "but you can come in and check if you want to."

She grinned and replied, "In your dreams, buddy."

Marvin laughed and said, "For all you know I could still be dreaming."

Mary laughed with him but added, "Listen, you got a message from George and he wants you to call as soon as soon as possible."

Marvin's hands stopped in mid-air as he was massaging his head with shampoo. "What did he say?"

"He said to tell you that both guys were definitely the same man…whatever that means."

Frowning, he asked her, "Did he tell you anymore?"

"No," she stated, "But he did say to call him at home when you were able."

Chief turned off the water and opened the shower curtain. Mary was there, ready with a towel. He grabbed it and leaned over and gave her a quick peck on the cheek. "I hope you have some coffee left, because I think I'm going to need it."

Playfully, he reached for her as she quickly scampered from the bathroom.

"You'd better have that coffee before you call him back. I want to have you to myself for once."

He smiled, "Okay, I'm on my way."

She yelled as she went down the hall towards the kitchen, "I'll be waiting!"

Claire trudged down the muddy, icy trail, growing more and more uncertain that this was the way she should be headed. *Let's see. I know this leads to the lake but I'm not sure if this is the right path. I'm looking for an old dock, one that has a canoe tipped upside down, laying next to it. From what Libby showed me it's still there.*

She looked ahead, trying to get her bearings. Her steps slowed down as she concentrated on her surroundings. *This doesn't look like it. I wonder if I went to the wrong parking area after all. I thought that was where Dad and I used to park his car, but now I'm beginning to remember another parking lot further down, off the main road.*

She stopped and looked around. *I'm sure of it! This is not the right area.*

She turned around to head back to the car but hesitated and thought, *maybe I'd better just continue this way. I'll probably have to go around the lake, and that might take longer, but I'm already half-way there anyway.*

Claire resumed her progress on the path. *Yeah, I need to get there as fast as I can. Libby is waiting for me.*

CHAPTER TWENTY-SIX

After talking to George for several minutes, Chief Hennessey sat at the kitchen table, sipping his coffee, not saying a word. Knowing from many years of experience that it was best not to disrupt his concentration, Mary waited patiently until he finally spoke.

"My retirement has been put on hold for a while, Mary."

She started to sputter, but before she could object, Marvin put up his hand. "Let me explain first."

She rolled her eyes but sat down next to him at the table and put her hands on the placemat. She started to fidget with the edges, which was an unconscious habit she had, but she sat there stoically expecting him to tell her why.

"We had a murder last night. It relates to a case that we've been working on for several years. George and I had just gone to see this man at the office where he works yesterday afternoon, and after we left, someone killed him."

Mary stared at him, sadness evident on her face, wary, but knowing he would unfold the story for her...and he did.

"Do you remember the deaf woman who disappeared four years ago?"

Mary nodded her head up and down once and asked, "Didn't you think that she might have gone off somewhere to escape her ex-husband, or to make a new life for herself in a different part of the country?"

Chief nodded affirmatively and said, "Yes, that's what we all thought, but it looks like her former husband might have had something to do with this murder last night. He worked at that trucking company and was there when George and I left yesterday afternoon." But that's not the only thing," he added.

"You think he killed his wife too?"

Marvin put his hand over hers, "How did you get so smart?"

She grabbed his hand and squeezed it affectionately, "I'm married to a cop...a darn good one...and he's not going to let this one get away either. I can tell you that!" She picked up his hand and kissed it.

He used his other hand to gently touch her hair, brushing it away from her eyes. "Haven't I always told you how you're always right?"

Dropping his hand, he hesitated before adding, "Plus, it looks like this guy has more than one identity, and it's very possible that he's killed more than these two."

Mary pulled back and waited for him to explain.

After listening to a summary of the phone conversation George Stanley had had with her husband, she was caught off guard when he concluded with an ominous statement.

"We don't know how yet, but this guy knows Claire Dungarven. He used her name as a reference on his application to Landry Trucking Company. It could be a sick joke, but even if it is, I need to find out if she knows him and if not, how would he know who she is and why would he use her name?"

"Maybe he read about her in the newspaper and has become obsessed with her," Mary offered.

"That's what I'm worried about."

The two of them sat quietly, pouring over the possibilities. Finally Mary asked, "Have you called her yet?"

Marvin sighed, "Yes, I tried calling her last night. She wasn't home but I left a message and I thought she would have called me back by now."

Mary's hand flew up to her mouth and she squealed, "I forgot. The phone rang and I didn't answer it. I thought you needed the sleep." She turned around and glanced at the phone. "Have you checked any messages yet?"

Marvin jumped up and grabbed the phone. He could hear the message beep signaling a call. "I didn't even think to check when I called George. I was so wrapped up in hearing what he had to tell me." He quickly punched in his number code. He stood there by the counter, listening intently. Mary held her breath. When he finally put the receiver down, Marvin remained quiet for what seemed an eternity.

Not able to squelch her anxiety any longer, Mary asked, "Well, what did she say?"

Chief continued to stand at the counter, frowning, silent.

"Marvin, what did she say?"

"It wasn't Claire, Mary. It was Jim Hoppes. He was at her house."

"But she got your message and she's okay, right?" She looked at him eagerly, awaiting reassurance.

He spoke in an almost dead tone of voice, "She's not there. She went to Pine Lake to find Libby Newman's body."

"Oh, my God," Mary uttered in shocked astonishment.

"Jim went to find her…and he wants me to come too."

"But, Marvin, why do you have to go? Can't Jim take care of it himself?" She pleaded.

"Mary," he sighed, "you don't understand."

She stood up, walked over to him, and grabbed his arm. "What don't I understand, Marvin?"

"Jim didn't tell me how he knows, but…."

She grasped his arm tighter, "but, what?"

"He told me that Libby's killer will be there too."

Why would she leave without me? Jim gripped the steering wheel tightly while cautiously monitoring the remaining ice ruts and mounds on the road. The sun was slowly doing its job but Jim didn't want to take any chances and wind up in a slide. All of his senses were keyed up and his focus was on finding Claire.

A car followed him at a discreet distance. The driver glared straight ahead; his focus was on Jim Hoppes and where his destination would take them. But he too was driving very carefully, and not because of the road conditions. His intent was to stay as invisible as possible. He didn't want to give away his identity just yet. He was following a police officer and had to be extra vigilant that he was not detected.

Trent reached over and touched the knife lying on the passenger seat. Was it uneasiness? Who knows, but a smile lit up his face when he fingered the knife. Was he imagining what it would do? A lack of conscience could make him do a lot of things that don't make sense to most people. Conscience is the antithesis of killing. And this murderer had nothing but more killing on his mind.

I hope it's not too late. A nagging voice entered his stream of thought and Jim quickly shut it down.

I know where she went. I just wish I could hurry it up!

Before turning on to highway 46 west out of Nashtown, Jim glanced over at the new Law Enforcement building and thought briefly about stopping to garner some help from Sheriff Wayne. He knew Ken would be expecting him to call or stop by to bring him up-to-date, but Jim didn't want to take the time to explain the latest twist in the case. He smiled wryly when he imagined how the sheriff would react to a ghost story. *Better continue on myself.*

As he drove on, he frowned at the thought of what might happen. *Claire is putting herself in a precarious position.*

Jim pushed down on the accelerator as soon as he left the small town and saw the speed limit sign indicating a higher speed was now in order.

As soon as he saw Jim Hoppes turn, Trent Newman knew exactly where they were headed. *He's going to Pine Lake!* He grimaced at the thought.

She must know! His expression took on a puzzling look. *But how did she find out?*

148

Reaching over, he fingered the knife for security. *It doesn't matter. Once she sees me, she'll forget about Libby.* Trent smiled at the thought. *She'll be so thrilled to see me again; she won't even give her a second thought!*

His heart started to beat faster. A sense of urgency made his brain kick in to overdrive as well. *I need to get to her before he does.*

He remembered a short cut to the Lake and smiled as he saw Jim speed past it. *Now I can get there ahead of him! When Claire sees me, she won't have any interest in Jim Hoppes!*

Trent let go of the knife and put his hand up to his mouth to squelch a giggle. *Then, Jim Hoppes will be 'history'... in more ways than one.*

Retired Captain Marvin Hennessey sat in his car, feeling the familiar bulge of his Glock, 9 mm. model 17, medium frame, in his holster, under his jacket. He turned the key in the ignition and smiled wryly at the now somewhat distant thought of retirement. *Guess it's been postponed.*

He had a worried expression on his face as he backed the car out of the driveway. *What's important is getting to Claire before someone tries to hurt her.*

His foot instinctively lowered on the gas pedal and speed picked up as he drove out of his neighborhood. *I hope Jim gets there before the killer does.*

He shook his head and thought, *who are we kidding? We know who the killer is. Why don't I just say it! Trent Newman! He's the killer and I can only hope that he's still out of town.*

Marvin eased out into traffic and slowed down impatiently to adjust to the beginning of afternoon commute. *But, what if he isn't?*

He found himself chafing at the volume of cars on the interstate as he dealt with the magnitude of the situation without his state-issued patrol car, which he had left at home, not wanting Trent Newman to see him following in it.

I'm finding out what it will be like to be an ordinary citizen again, he thought as a sardonic smile touched his lips.

Chief eased over into the far left lane and watched as drivers found their way to their exits at some of the more populated areas on the south side of Indianapolis. Heavily placing his foot down on the accelerator, he pushed the speed limit and steadily drove toward his destination. The exit to Columbus would take him to Pine Lake. *Wish there was a faster way to get there!* Feeling his impatience growing, he breathed deeply and concentrated on what lay ahead. The early spring setting sun glimmered in the west; light tones of pink and salmon adding to its beauty, but Marvin Hennessey didn't really notice. His mind was on his journey…and where it might take him.

Claire trudged along on the path that would eventually take her to the site she remembered, the one that would hopefully hold the truth about what had happened to Libby Newman. She too saw the setting sun and didn't let its beauty deter her, but she automatically quickened her steps out of a sudden sense of urgency at beating the dark before it came to her. Instinctively she knew that finding Libby would be much safer for her if dusk hadn't settled in. Night made for enough shadows on its own. It held mystery, but also brought fear, especially if faced alone.

Worriedly, she watched the sky as the tinges of color turned stark and foreboding, pale pink giving way to deep orange, and then to rust as the sun settled deeper into its palette. While others might be watching this sequence with a sense of awe and appreciation of breathtaking natural charm, Claire had the temerity to import a certain amount of fear into her reaction, a fear bred from anticipation, anticipation caused by the fear of the unknown. And so the cycle went…fear, anticipation, more fear, and the unknown.

It had a certain cadence to it as she walked, ironically reminding her of one of her favorite movies. She smiled, remembering watching the "Wizard of Oz" and hearing Judy Garland saying over and over again as she walked, 'Lions and tigers and bears…oh, my! Lions and tigers and bears…oh, my!'

She resisted the urge to say it aloud and instead proclaimed, "Libby, if you're there, I'm coming."

Afraid someone might have seen her and wondered why she was talking to herself in the middle of the woods, she ducked her head shyly and looked around. Glancing over her shoulder and to each side, she breathed a sigh of relief when she realized she was entirely alone in the woods this late afternoon going into early evening time. Her police instincts were focusing on the task at hand and not the inherent danger that might be involved.

Better pay attention to where I'm going. Don't want to forget my way back even though I think this is the right path. I'll do well to concentrate on remembering some of the landmarks.

Then, she made a point of taking in her surroundings, and she noticed details that started to come back to her. *I remember that bench with the crude writing on it--'Larry' and then a big heart and 'Kris'.*

Remembering her own teenage years, Claire kept occupied for the next few minutes thinking about some of the foolish things she and her boyfriends would do to show their love for each other. *Sex wasn't part of the equation—not until you were engaged or married. Nowadays, kids aren't as simple as that.*

She shook her head, *too bad they don't consider the consequences. They might be facing a lifetime of regret for making a wrong decision.*

"Oh well, I can't solve the problems of this generation; I can't even solve mine," she said as she continued walking, her mind back on following Libby's and her own leads.

There's the turn off. I remember this bend.

Claire stopped and seemed to be considering something. "That's where the other parking area is!" She pointed to the opposite footpath that approached the bend.

"That's the way we used to come!"

Garnering her thoughts, she smiled and said, "No wonder, it took me so long. If I had remembered the other path, I would have been here a lot quicker."

She continued down to the lake, noting identifying marks as she walked, *there's the big, old, gnarly oak tree with the large branch I used to sit on while my Dad fished.*

Hmm, the ground is barren where the melting snow doesn't cover it. Looks like people might build fires here now. Too bad.

Back then, Dad wasn't close enough to keep an eye on me, but he could hear me singing my favorite song—'Love Letters in the sand'. Boy, did I have a crush on Pat Boone when I was a kid!

Claire grinned to herself as she plodded along, closer and closer to her destination. *There's the tree stump I used to sit on, the clearing where Dad and I would put our things. Sometimes he would bring along a small tent on hot summer days. We'd pitch it right there and eat our picnic inside if it rained.*

Her mind raced, happily bringing up old memories, taking in the now familiar surroundings. Her pace quickened as the excitement of the past came back to her, yet she came to an abrupt halt when the lake loomed into view.

Her steps resumed, although at a slower rate. She saw the weeds encroaching on the open dirt space leading to the water; an old canoe was tipped over next to the dock; and the dock was listing to one side, half in and half out of the lake, not very stable and obviously not in use anymore.

Where the ice had started to break up, water lapped up against the sides of the canoe, making whooshing noises, almost like it was trumpeting Claire's arrival. It beckoned her, but in an unfriendly, non-welcoming way.

She hesitated and almost turned around, but instantly a picture of Libby entered her mind and she stood still, gathering her strength before going into the clearance. Simultaneously, the night moved in and everything turned black.

CHAPTER TWENTY-SEVEN

As the last streaks of sunset gave way to the more sinister shaded sky, Trent Newman carefully turned into the Pine Lake Recreational Area. He took in the environment and noticed no cars, no people, not even park rangers.

Under cover of darkness...no witnesses to worry about, he thought. *All I need is to concentrate on where I'm going.*

He smiled in anticipation of the fateful meeting he had planned for Claire. *Finally, the love of my life is here!*

Grinning from ear to ear, he reasoned, *In fact, what a great place to make it all happen!*

As Trent recalled what had occurred here four years ago, a frown replaced his smile, *How did Claire know to come here?*

Agitated, he continued questioning, *does she suspect Libby is buried here? And, if so, who else might know my secret?*

He thought about Jim Hoppes and frowned. Trent knew that he would have to kill him if that was the case. He clutched the knife tighter, squeezing the handle as if it was a replacement for a future victim's neck.

Responding to the building uneasiness, Trent applied more pressure on the accelerator as he followed the main road into the park. Rounding a curve, he did not see another car turn into the entrance. All of his attention was focused on finding Claire.

He knew she would understand. *It had always been about Claire.* He loved her and no one else.

There's her car! He recognized immediately that she had parked in the wrong lot.

This buys me more time, if she hasn't been here long.

Again, his grin turned to a scowl. *But, if she has, I don't want her digging around too much. She might be sorry if she finds anything.*

Trent continued on to the right parking lot. Organizing his thoughts and preparing for what he would tell Claire, he didn't notice the other car as it pulled into the same parking area she had used.

❖

As Jim Hoppes approached the park, he noticed a vehicle turning onto the main road and deliberately slowed down to make himself less visible. Jim strained his eyes to see the other car and identify its occupant.

Can't tell for sure, but it looks like a man driving. Hard to see more than that...he hesitated and remembered something...*it was following me on 46 and turned off on a side road behind me.*

His analytical mind struggled to remember anything else of importance, and his eyes lit up when he finally recalled that that road led to Pine Lake too. *Now I remember! It's a short cut to the Lake!*

Jim pushed himself to recollect when he first noticed the vehicle behind him. *I know it wasn't behind me when I drove through Nashville, but maybe he was trying to follow at a distance.*

The car doesn't ring a bell...or does it?

He fought to recall more details. *Whoever it is he stayed too far back for me to make a positive I.D., so now I'd best be careful, stay back, and keep an eye on him.*

No one else is in the Park that I can see so why would anyone be here? It's almost dark, still cold...not exactly a prime time for picnicking.

Then, a look of determination came over Jim's face as he realized his suspicions might be warranted. *I'll follow at a safe distance with my lights turned off. Don't want to alert him to my presence. He might be up to no good.*

Jim let his foot off the accelerator and slowed down. Turning off his headlights before rounding the curve, he kept his eyes on the car ahead. *Hmmm...wonder why the person driving that car slowed and braked slightly?*

The other car sped up again almost as if he had read Jim's mind. *Guess I'll find out soon enough.*

As Jim kept an eye on the car lights ahead, he came to the point in the road where the other driver had slowed down and braked. Jim looked over. *That's Claire's car!*

Without hesitating he made a fateful decision and swung his car into the same parking area.

Claire stood there in the clearing, her eyes adjusting to nightfall, taking in the details while her mind absorbed the visual memories. She listened to the sounds of nature and surroundings and could hear the canoe bobbing up and down in the slight current, tapping against the rickety dock. An owl hooted in the distance. Claire thought she heard a small animal skitter across the forest floor, but the hard ground muted the sound enough to cast some doubt on her auditory impression.

Feeling foolish now and wondering how she planned to summon up a ghost, she leaned against one of the dock posts and thought, *so, what's next, Claire Dungarven? Do you wait until Libby appears or do you say something and alert her to the fact that you're here?*

Claire shook her head. *That's pretty silly. She's the one who told me to come! She's here and she knows I am too!*

Sighing, she stood up straight and announced to the cold and dark, "Libby, it's Claire. If you're here, please let me know."

Looking obliquely out over the lake, her senses sharpened as she tried to pick up any noise or vision that would herald Libby's presence. Starting to doubt her own sanity, she positioned herself there in that spot to stare out into the night, almost in a hypnotic trance. She didn't realize that she was hardly breathing until she let out a strong exhalation. And that was the exact moment when she heard a tenuous rustling coming from the forest behind her. Tensing, she listened with all the inner strength she could muster.

Her ears hurt physically from the strain she put on herself, but no other sound emanated from the woods.

Claire couldn't identify the noise because it was so hushed as to be inconsequential. However she knew it wasn't. It was there and it was there for a reason. It was alerting her to a presence and she knew in that instant that she was about to meet Libby Newman face-to-face.

She turned around slowly, feeling the trepidation, hearing her own heart hammering away inside her chest. Her eyes focused on the outlines coming into sight—the stoic tree trunks, spreading out into barren branches, with moonlight filtering through. But as Claire adjusted her eyesight to take in the surroundings of land and not water, she was hit with the vision of a shape forming amongst the trees. It seemed to take on more substance as it moved forward out of the forest and into the space between solid and liquid, between woods and lake. Was it just her mind playing tricks on her or did it look like it was floating as it approached? Her brain didn't have time to answer that question before she jolted upright in surprising recognition of the figure before her as night glow lit up the features. Shock coursed through her body and she shivered as the night air turned even colder. Her eyes opened wide and her hand flew up to cover her mouth as she said, "Oh my God, what are <u>you</u> doing here?"

CHAPTER TWENTY-EIGHT

"Surprised to see me?"

Claire stood perfectly still, stunned with the dawning realization that the figure approaching her was not a ghost, but the rock-hard, solid substance of a man...and one whom she remembered from her past. Assessing his face, she could see that the span of time had not been kind to him. As she looked closer, she realized that it was not just the years gone by, but also a frame of mind, maybe a personality quirk that she had never noticed before, that especially affected his countenance.

Overall, it gave him an aspect that was not pleasing to the eye. In fact, it seemed to bring out the worst type of characteristics that might be found in a person—deep, rigid lines that ran across the face, not the kind that were earned, but the ones that sprung forth from within, signaling an evil that had been artfully and purposefully hidden, seemingly at will. As Claire continued to stare, she shuddered inwardly at the false expectations of the past and the frightening reality of the present.

"I...I'm just in shock. It's been a long, long time."

"Ahh, yes it has, Claire, but I've never been far away. I've kept up with you," he said, grinning expansively.

She smiled in return, but all the while she was attempting to gauge his intent and study his features more closely. *Same determined set to his jaw line, but now it looks leaner and meaner to me.*

Mistaking her smile for an invitation to come closer, he edged nearer.

She noticed the slim, but muscular body. *A little softer around the edges, but that happens with age.*

"You're checking me out, aren't you?" He laughed heartily, but to Claire's ears it sounded sinister.

A growing repulsion caused her stomach to jerk. She focused on hiding her observations…and the dislike that was building inside.

Buying time, she spoke up. "You've not told me yet why you're here." She forced another smile.

"Why Claire, I think you're glad to see me. I bet you've missed me." He moved to within an arm's link of her.

Then, she looked into his eyes and gasped.

He grabbed her a little too forcefully and she blurted out, "What happened to your eyes?"

His grip loosened slightly on her arms and he said, "Why, whatever do you mean, dear Claire? I thought you loved my eyes." He stared darkly into her face.

Knowing that she didn't need to anger him right now, she responded, "Oh, nothing really. I just thought they were green; now they're brown." She gritted her teeth and added, "Very attractive though…just different."

He laughed loudly and hugged her. "Just like you, Claire. You don't miss a thing, do you? Contacts are so useful, don't you think," he added. "You can be whoever you want to be." He bent his head to look at her.

She attempted a giggle but it came out more like a strangled cry when she suddenly realized that she couldn't reach her gun without a struggle. *Better try to keep him occupied so I can get him to share some details with me.* She worked furiously to control the burgeoning fear that threatened to spill over and make itself evident to him.

"And, who are you?" Claire asked flippantly. Her head pounded with the beginning of a terrible headache as she awaited his answer.

He gazed longingly at her, as seconds ticked away, before blurting out, "Why I'm a regular chameleon, darlin'…to you I'm Greg Roberts… but to others I'm Trent Newman."

Claire inhaled deeply with surprise, but at the same time fought the strong urge to scream. *How could I have missed it?*

Her mind spun dizzily out of control. Scenes from the past came back at her like a kaleidoscope, blurry at first, but with dawning clarity as she saw in her mind's eye the manifest signs that should have been there all along: *same build, color of hair, features...just hardened.* Her eyes widened in shock. *Why didn't I recognize him? Was it just because he changed his eye color?*

She remembered then, *I didn't interview him! Brad Peters did that part of the investigation. I saw the mug shot but it wasn't very good...he wore a cap.* She mentally slapped herself for not paying closer attention to the picture.

Then, we decided that we didn't have enough evidence to even make the determination that she was dead so we left it at that.

Forcing herself to recover as quickly as possible, she replied, "Why, Greg? Why all the mystery? 'Why the different identities? What's your reason for all this?"

He glared at her with distrust; he didn't care for the barrage of questions but he contained his seething anger and quietly responded, "It's all been for you, Claire. I love you and have always loved you, but you left me when you found out I was married, right?" He shook her shoulders and she winced in pain.

"But you didn't have to kill someone, Greg." Claire's eyes glistened with tears.

Greg let her go but remained close by her side. "Which one," he said quietly.

She stood still for a minute as the realization of what he had just said hit her.

Tremulously she asked, "Which one? What do you mean by that? Do you mean there were others?"

His voice remained calm but she could see his body tense, his arms by his side, hands opening and closing into fists. He stood ramrod straight and hesitated before answering in a patronizing tone, "Of course there were others, Claire. You were my one and only love and I couldn't share you with anyone."

Alarmed and confused, she questioned, "What do you mean 'you couldn't share me with anyone?"

Greg laughed again and relaxed now. He leaned against the dock post, his attention on the lapping water as it came onto the lake's shore. His eyes took on a thoughtful but evil glare; at that moment he seemed to make the impromptu decision to tell his story, not to unburden himself, but to relish in what he saw as his accomplishments.

He folded his arms. "You know the most fun was running over that policeman boyfriend of yours. I couldn't believe my luck! I'd been following him for days and I knew his route and routine." He secretly stole a glance at Claire, looked back at the water's edge, and continued, "When I saw him stop that guy for speeding, I knew it was time to act. I turned around in the median, came up from behind, and plowed right into him." Greg smiled at the memory, "He didn't have a chance. He was dead before he hit the ground."

Claire was listening to all of this with a mixture of shock and outrage. Nausea hit the pit of her stomach. Tears started flowing freely down her cheeks. She struggled to control her composure so she could gather more details from this monster...and buy some time... but the hatred she now felt kept interfering.

Impulsively, she shouted, "How could you do that, Greg? What did he do to you?"

Greg turned his head to look at her and wickedly said, "Why, Claire, he tried to take you away from me. I couldn't have that."

It was an absurd justification that mentally ill people sometimes use, but Claire saw it for what it was—sheer evil.

Her fear was growing by the second, but she plied him with questions, using the time to study a way she could catch him off-guard. "Why did you kill Libby, Greg? Was it because she divorced you?" Her voice nearly strangled on the last part. She was hoping he didn't notice and see right through her feigned interest.

"No. True, we got a divorce, but that wasn't why."

She persisted, "Then, why?"

He looked at her with disdain and sarcastically said, "I wanted you back and I was afraid you might not be happy with my past matrimonies." And then he added, "Because, if that had been the case, my dear Claire, you might have thought badly of me."

Ignoring the biting response, her mind raced, flooding with details from the past. She blurted out, "Libby was your second wife! You were married to someone else when I knew you."

Greg snarled and replied, "Smart bitch, aren't you?"

Claire thought about her gun, but he was standing too close. And, he was on her right side which was where her gun was. She saw him put his hand in his pocket and noticed a faint glint of steel protruding. Thinking quickly, she softly asked him another question, "Did you kill her, Greg? Did you do that for me too?"

He grinned and looked at her closely as if to gauge her emotional response before deciding she was trustworthy and said, "She was smart too, Claire."

He paused again as he considered her reasons for wanting to know and her acceptance of what he was saying. Internally he must have decided that she was being sincere so he continued, "I met you a year after I changed my identity the first time. Up until that time I was Grady Rogers, truck driver, married, and no children, living in Brown County. Eight years ago my wife and I had some financial problems."

He paused; this part of the story always made him mad. "She was a selfish, greedy woman...always wanting more...never satisfied with the money I brought home from my trucking job." He sneered, "of course, she didn't want to work; she just wanted me to make more money!"

As Claire watched, Greg continued to finger the knife in his pocket. She pressed him for more details. "What did she want? You had a nice house, didn't you?"

He replied with emotion, "Yes, we had a nice house! In fact we lived in Sweetwater, same as you. But she was never satisfied. She wanted more." He spat on the ground in a visible show of disgust for her avarice.

"So what did you do?"

"Funny, she went along with me on that one." He sighed and seemed lost in thought before resuming, "I brought a hitchhiker home from one of my road trips. We had a nice, long talk in the truck. He was homeless, didn't have any family, and was on his way to Florida for the winter. I suggested he spend the night with us and I'd drive him to the interstate the next morning after he got a good night's sleep in a real bed for a change." Greg grinned as he remembered that part. "And, I promised him a home-cooked meal." He laughed. "I think that's what did the trick. Bastard hadn't eaten in a couple of days. Didn't take much to talk him into it."

"What happened to him?"

He stared off into space, his eyes as dark as the night sky. "Killed him; hit him over the head with a shovel and then I burned the house down to cover it up," Greg replied flatly.

Claire swallowed a shriek when she recognized his story. She squeezed her eyes shut and quietly asked, "Why'd you kill him? What happened after that?"

"After he went to bed, my wife...her name was Doris...we talked and I told her about this great idea to make some money." He stifled a laugh and continued, "She liked it as much as I did! After he went to sleep, I went into the bedroom and hit him several times. Then I burned the house down; she ran from the house to the neighbor's and I ran into the woods; end of story."

Claire watched Greg's face. He seemed lost in his own thoughts. She thought briefly about going for her gun but he still had a hand on the knife. She decided to stall him by asking for more details. "That's not the end of the story. Was the fire ruled an arson? Did they think you died in the fire? Where is Doris, Greg?"

"Why Claire, if I didn't know you better, I'd think you were enjoying this," he taunted her.

She could tell by the tone of his voice that she'd better be careful. Meekly, she responded, "No, I'm just curious." She made an effort to look at him with as much sincerity as she could muster and asked, "What did happen next, Greg?"

He examined Claire's face for any signs of deception and then convinced himself that she was truly interested because he opened his mouth to speak. But, before he could respond, Greg thought he heard a noise in the woods and hesitated. His ears perked up and he listened intently. Subconsciously his hand tightened its grip on the knife.

In close proximity, Claire noticed the subtle movement of his hand and held her breath in response. She did not hear the noise.

Greg listened for a few more minutes before answering her question. Hearing nothing more, he proceeded with his story.

"The fire was ruled an arson. The firemen found the body but it was burned beyond recognition. They believed it was me. Doris said I'd come home late and didn't want to disturb her so I went to sleep in the guest bedroom. They thought I was smoking in bed and caused the fire." He snickered as if this was all just an example of dark humor.

Claire shuddered at his callous disregard for life, but forced herself to urge him on. "What happened then?"

Even though Greg seemed reluctant to reply, he only paused for a minute before answering, "Doris had what was left cremated and buried." His voice was devoid of any emotion.

He heaved a sigh and said, "After that, she moved to a different house in Brown County. I'd come to see her when I wasn't on the road but I had to hide in case the cops paid her a visit…and believe me, they did."

He stared off into the dark night for what seemed an eternity before continuing, "She sure wasn't happy when the insurance company refused to give her a settlement right away." He frowned and added, "She finally got her settlement last year when the seven years were up and the state declared me legally dead. She moved to Tennessee because it was safer for me to visit her there. No one was suspicious. No one there knew us well enough to ask questions."

Claire looked at him questioningly. "Who was that woman I saw you with at the bookstore then?"

Greg smiled wickedly and replied, "So, that's when you realized I was married. You saw me with her! Now I see!"

"Who was she?"

"Jealous?"

Claire persisted, "Who was she?"

"That was Doris," Greg responded. His voice had a flat, monotone quality to it.

Claire's heart was hammering so loudly that she assumed he could hear it.

"We took a chance and she came along with me on a road trip. We stopped in just to buy her a book to read. She was always wanting to read." He glowered and continued, "It made me nervous to go there but she insisted."

He shook his head in disgust, "I should have known that was what happened, but when you wouldn't call me back, I just figured you were seeing someone else...like that ex-boyfriend of yours...Doug."

Claire resisted the urge to scream back in anger at him. She asked him quietly, "When did you meet Libby?"

"She came into my life shortly after you broke up with me."

Claire wanted to lash out and slap him for continuing to blame her for everything, but she held her emotions in check once again.

"I met her at a class I was taking," Greg explained. "I liked taking adult education classes; I could meet pretty women there too, just like at bookstores," he added, grinning at Claire.

She resisted his taunting and calmly waited for him to continue the story.

"She was there with her interpreter. I remembered a little sign language from when I was a kid and I went up to her at one of the classes. She was pretty and seemed to like me. I asked her out for coffee and she accepted. We started dating and the rest is history."

Claire knew these details from the investigation but continued to ply him with questions to buy some time. "But weren't you still married to Doris?"

Greg laughed. "Again Claire, you amaze me. Yes, I was still married but that wasn't a problem. Hey, I'm a truck driver! I realized I could lead any life I wanted to!"

He added, "And, after Doris had me declared legally dead, she wasn't useful to me anymore, so I killed her too."

Claire gasped. She grappled with the sheer magnitude of what he was telling her, but managed to ask, "Is that why you killed Libby, Greg…because she wasn't useful to you anymore?"

Quietly he responded, "She was upset with me. She never knew about Doris, but she didn't like the long absences that truck driving can cause. She filed for divorce because she was lonely."

"Then why did you have to kill her, Greg?"

He sighed, "Believe it or not, I loved her. I went to see her one night and I convinced her to come for a motorcycle ride with me. I parked at a utility substation close to the house. We walked over there, got on the cycle, and left…," his voice trailed off.

"But she didn't mean you any harm, Greg."

His head snapped around and he glared at Claire. "Oh yes she did!"

"How do you know that?"

"She was going to abandon me too, Claire. She was planning to move out to California. No one knew that but me. She told me after she lost out on another promotion at work. We kept in touch you know," he added. "I wanted her to stay but she wouldn't do it. She'd made up her mind."

"So, why would you kill her, Greg?" Claire tried her best to be noncommittal.

"I couldn't take a chance. She'd already told me she was going to quit that next week and move. She was planning to leave me, just like you, and I wanted her to stay."

Claire noted that his voice took on an almost childish, pleading quality to it.

Snap! Both of them fell quiet when they heard the sound in the trees behind them. Greg grabbed Claire with one hand and slid the knife out of his pocket with the other. He spun her around so they both faced the woods, placed the knife so that it was touching the small of her back and said, "Whoever you are come out and show yourself or she dies!"

Claire remained perfectly still, her breathing quick and erratic. Seconds felt like minutes; minutes felt like hours. Nothing stirred.

"I mean it! You'd better come out now!"

Claire strained to see into the forest. She jumped when she saw a shape step out from behind the large oak tree. She felt the knife press harder against her back. The figure moved closer. Her knees went wobbly and she almost fainted when she recognized who it was.

CHAPTER TWENTY-NINE

"Let her go, Trent." The form continued to advance, holding a gun in his hand while he spoke. "Let her go right now or I'll shoot."

A sinister smile crossed Trent's face. "Now why would I do that?" After all, Jim, I'm the one with a knife in her back. Do you want to take a chance and watch her die?" Jim Hoppes hesitated slightly and Trent continued, "Drop the gun or I'll kill her."

"Do what he says, Jim."

He looked in her eyes and saw the pleading; he also saw something else. Her eyes traveled down to her right side and her head dipped ever so meaningfully.

Trent didn't feel or see the scant movement. His attention was squarely on Jim. He repeated what Claire said in a sarcastic tone. "Yes, Jim. Do what he says." He twisted her arm until she moaned in pain.

Hearing this, Jim let the gun fall to the ground in front of him. He raised his hands in surrender and said, "Okay, just let her go."

"Oooh, sounds like Jim cares about you, Claire." He put his head down and nuzzled the side of her face. "That might not be too good for him."

Alarmed, Claire burst out, "Don't hurt him, Greg. Let him go. I'll stay with you."

Before he could reply, Jim spoke up. "Why did you call him 'Greg', Claire?"

"Tell him," he ordered her.

"He's both, Jim. He's Trent Newman but I remember him as Greg Roberts."

"And, you might remember me as Grady Rogers," Trent added.

Startled, Jim stared closer. Shocked, he quietly whispered, "Grady Rogers! Oh my God! It is you! I thought you might still be alive!"

"You won't be for long, though."

"He killed his first wife, Doris Rogers. He killed Libby too," Claire said to Jim.

Trent twisted her arm again more forcefully than before and Claire gritted her teeth so as not to scream out in pain.

Jim clenched his fists and bent forward in response to the pain evident on Claire's face. He started to say something but remained quiet when he sensed a change in the atmosphere; it almost felt like another person was present.

Claire and Trent were silent too as a noticeable chill in the air seemed to spread out and cause the already frigid night to become even more frozen. But, it was more than just the cold that hushed them, and they all stood still as that sense of another presence suddenly invaded their space. It wasn't a noise this time, but only a feeling that came over them as they stood in the clearing adjacent to the lake. In the night air they experienced a frost that went beyond a winter evening breeze. The iciness heralded the proximity of a being, even though no one was visible in the darkness.

Claire could feel Trent tighten his grip on the knife. He stood quietly, watchful, with an uneasiness that mirrored the soundlessness. She and Jim shared a questioning glance. Unspoken, it denoted an uncertainty of what it was they were all feeling.

Finally, in their increasingly clear night vision, they could see a shape beginning to form a short distance from them in the woods. It was fuzzy at first, only an outline. As it began to take on the appearance of something more solid, all three inhaled sharply as they simultaneously realized that they were looking at the ghost of Libby Newman.

She held her arm out in front of her and pointed to Trent. Then she swung her arm around and pointed into the woods, sadly gazing at a spot between two pine trees. Snow covered the ground but as Libby continued to focus on this location, water and then blood started to ooze up out of the ground, bubbling, gathering momentum and volume, until it turned the earth a rust color. It moved closer to the threesome as it threatened to overtake the landscape.

Startled and frightened, Trent gasped and Claire could feel his grasp on the knife weaken tenuously. But both of them, and Jim, felt as if something or someone was holding them in place. Their bodies were paralyzed.

Then, Libby pushed into the consciousness of each one present, the true story of her death. Through wordless pictures she showed them how Trent came to see her at the house and begged and beseeched her not to leave him and move to California.

She impressed upon them her stubbornness and refusal to bend to his wishes. She gave them a sense of her desire to flee and make a better life for herself.

Fast forwarding, Libby showed them how Trent convinced her to go with him for one last ride on his motorcycle. She loved riding with him...and he knew that. She enjoyed the freedom of riding, hair blowing in the breeze, feeling the pull of the great beyond. Not able to resist, and unaware that this would be her last ride, she walked with him to where he had parked his motorcycle and hopped on the back. Libby was not concerned when Trent drove into Pine Lake; that was one of their favorite spots when they were together.

The thoughts that were being impressed into Trent, Jim and Claire's minds turned dark and menacing as Libby approached the climax of the story. They all felt a pounding in their heads as she revealed the last minutes of her life.

The images came fast and furious. Trent argued. He tried to persuade Libby to stay. He wanted her back. She shook her head, 'no' and turned to walk back to the motorcycle. He pulled out the knife and started stabbing her over and over again. His rage continued unabated for several seconds until he stopped, took a breath, and bent over to look at her. He realized he had killed her. His passion had caused him to plunge the knife into her seven times. The last wound was the one that killed her. It struck her in the heart and Libby Newman breathed her last breath.

The dreamlike kaleidoscope Trent, Jim and Claire were seeing slowed down and the sadness of this moment was felt in all three. There was a pause, giving each an opportunity to experience the death of Libby Newman. Tears streamed down Claire's face. Jim bent his head in sorrow and silently said a prayer. Trent didn't move; shock and disbelief kept him rooted to the spot.

In slow motion the pictures started up again and showed how Trent used a shovel he had hidden in the old canoe to dig a burial place for Libby. He placed her body in the hole, covered it up and disguised it with dirt and leaves, deep enough for no one to discover in the last four years she had been gone.

Then, as a fitting conclusion, Libby turned and pointed to her grave again. On top of the ground were all the signs in the snow that had been left for Claire…a knife, a rose, and a shoeprint had all magically appeared in the mix of blood and water that continued to seep up through the soil.

Of course! Now it all makes sense! He used a knife to kill her and he buried her near water. She wanted me to know who was trying to communicate with me so she left the rose because she had a rose tattoo. Wordlessly, Claire sent a message of thanks to Libby and she smiled back in understanding.

Trent seemed unaware of the silent missive flowing between the two women. He remained frozen in fear. With his attention diverted, Claire stole a look at Jim and nodded slightly. Trent was so shaken by the ghostly image of Libby that he did not notice Jim bend over. In the next second, when he finally felt Claire shift unobtrusively, it was too late for him to regain his position of authority. A shot rang out and a body fell to the ground.

EPILOGUE

The small group huddled around a table at the State Police Post, drinking hot coffee, silently absorbing the facts as they came to light during their discussion.

Clark Tomlinson walked into the room and announced to all present. "Crime technicians are finished at the site. They found the grave and it looks like it could be her." Puzzled, he continued, "They found a knife and a rose on top of the ground...not sure if they were placed there by Trent or not." He shook his head and said, "They just called and will be here shortly...with everything." His voice trailed off as he turned and looked at Claire and Jim. They didn't respond, only sipped at their coffee, avoiding eye contact.

George Stanley swallowed and nodded his head up and down. "Thanks, Clark. We'll still be here when they arrive. Just tell them to come on in."

Officer Tomlinson softly closed the door behind him.

The group remained quiet for a few seconds and then, Claire spoke up in an obvious attempt to change the group's train of thought. "So, Chief," she paused as if still trying to get things straight in her mind. "Tell me again how you knew to come out to Pine Lake?"

Jim spoke up before he could answer. "I called him, Claire. I just wanted him to come along with me in case we had any trouble."

"And I didn't get the message until after Jim had left," Captain Hennessey interrupted. "But, I decided to follow him out there anyway."

Claire sighed, "Good thing you did, Marvin. You saved our lives."

"Yes, Chief, if you hadn't shot Trent Newman when you did, Claire and I might be dead right now."

"If you hadn't bent over to grab your gun when you did, Jim, I'd have shot you instead!"

The group around the table managed to smile at this bleak attempt at dark humor.

"But, I'm curious," Chief said. "How did you know this Trent Newman, Claire?"

"I had the misfortune to date the guy about eight years ago. I met him at a book store; we had a few dates and then I found out he was married."

"That was back when he was calling himself Greg Roberts, right?"

"Yeah, I didn't know it of course, but that was a false identity too."

Corporal Stanley spoke up next. "So, let's summarize what we know and get this straight. This guy was Grady Rogers. He and his wife committed a murder and then set their house on fire to collect on some insurance money?"

Claire responded affirmatively, "Yes, they used some poor homeless guy that Grady had picked up as a hitchhiker."

"Then, he disappeared for a while and resurfaced only to meet you, Claire, the love of his life..."

"Please, George, let's not play up that angle too much!"

"Okay, my apologies." He grinned and continued, "Grady, or Greg, figured out that you dumped him and then he took on the identity of Trent Newman, met Libby, and married her."

"And, he was still married to his first wife!" Jim shook his head in disbelief.

"Libby was suspicious of his long absences but just chalked it up to being a truck driver," Claire interjected.

"So," Marvin picked up the story, "she divorced him and then disappeared the next year."

"He said that she was planning to move to California...," Claire hesitated before reminding him, "We suspected that might be the case, remember?"

"Yes, I remember…and then he told you that he was afraid he might lose her, even though they were already divorced…and he killed her for that?"

"Crazy…but remember we were dealing with a psycho serial killer," Jim replied.

"And, he killed Doug for no reason at all," Claire added quietly.

Jim reached over and put his arm around her shoulder. "As I said, Claire, we had a nut case on our hands."

"Yeah, I know but it just seems so surreal. To think that he would kill so many people…he told me he killed his first wife after he found out that she had him declared legally dead. He felt she was of no use to him anymore," she lowered her head and paused, "I can't believe it. It's just too horrible to consider."

"We've all been in law enforcement long enough to know that loonies do crazy things," Corporal Stanley responded.

"Don't forget, George…he probably killed Art Cane too," Marvin said.

"Hell, we know he killed Mr. Cane!"

The group fell silent again.

Claire glanced at Jim surreptitiously. She hoped he caught her message—should we tell them about Libby?

He placed his hand over hers and squeezed. She nodded slightly and remained quiet.

Jim nonchalantly spoke up," Will you need us when the techs get here, George? Or, can we go home and get a few hours of sleep first?"

"I don't think it will do any harm for the two of you to get some rest first, Jim. Go on and we'll call you in the morning."

Claire smiled in gratitude. She stood up to leave and bent over to give Marvin a hug. "Thanks again, Chief."

He smiled up at her and whispered, "Thank Libby too, Claire."

She stiffened in shock and reared her head up to look Marvin in the eyes. She whispered, "Did you see her?"

He shrugged his shoulders and said, "Sometimes the night can play tricks on us."

She stared at him. An unspoken doubt hung in the air between them, but she saw the answer in his smile and in the discreet wink he gave her.

THE END

ABOUT THE AUTHOR

Jennifer Seet is the author of *Borderland* and now *Snow Signs*. Both are fictional paranormal thrillers set in the hills of southern Indiana. Jennifer is a retired teacher from the Indiana School for the Deaf, who lives in Brown County, Indiana, with her husband, Bob. She has always had a fascination for and even some personal experiences with the spirit world.

Mrs. Seet has also written professionally on the subject of Deaf Education and Autism, having two adult sons with the disability.

While working at the Indiana School for the Deaf, she wrote several short stories for a federally-funded literacy project for deaf children. When she started her writing career after retirement, her fellow teachers at the school urged her to include deaf characters in her books. *Snow Signs* is a first offering at fulfilling that promise to her dear friends at the school and in the Deaf community.

www.ingramcontent.com/pod-product-compliance
Lightning Source LLC
Chambersburg PA
CBHW030506260626
47157CB00005B/1670